Read more in the Hill School Girls series

Secrets
Strangers
Trouble

Read more for middle readers from Duckbill

Ninja Nani and the Bumbling Burglars by Lavanya Karthik
Ninja Nani and the Zapped Zombie Kids by Lavanya Karthik
Against All Odds by Ramendra Kumar
The Case of the Candy Bandit by Archit Taneja
The Case of the Careless Aliens by Archit Taneja
Oops the Mighty Gurgle by RamG Vallath
The Deadly Royal Recipe by Ranjit Lal
Vanamala and the Cephalopod by Shalini Srinivasan
Flat-track Bullies by Balaji Venkataramanan
Ravana Refuses to Die by Rustom Dadachanji
Dhanak by Anushka Ravishankar and Nagesh Kukunoor
Simply Nanju by Zainab Sulaiman
Hot Chocolate is Thicker than Blood by Rupa Gulab
The Sherlock Holmes Connection by Martin Widmark, Anushka Ravishankar, Katarina Genar and Bikram Ghosh
Tiger Boy by Mitali Perkins
Pops! by Balaji Venkataramanan
Karma Fights a Monster by Evan Purcell
Karma Meets a Zombie by Evan Purcell
Ninja Nani and the Mad Mummy Mix-up by Lavanya Karthik
Neha and the Nose by Ruchika Chanana
The Piano: Story of a Friendship by Nandita Basu

Alone

A. Coven

An imprint of Penguin Random House

DUCKBILL BOOKS

USA | Canada | UK | Ireland | Australia
New Zealand | India | South Africa | China | Singapore

Duckbill Books is part of the Penguin Random House group of companies whose addresses can be found at global.penguinrandomhouse.com

Published by Penguin Random House India Pvt. Ltd
4th Floor, Capital Tower 1, MG Road,
Gurugram 122 002, Haryana, India

Penguin Random House India

First published by Duckbill Books 2017

This edition published in Duckbill Books by Penguin Random House India 2020

10 9 8 7 6 5 4 3 2

ISBN 9789387103009

Typeset by PrePSol Enterprises Pvt. Ltd.

Printed at Repro India Limited

www.penguin.co.in

FSC www.fsc.org MIX Paper from responsible sources FSC® C047271

This is a legitimate digitally printed version of the book and therefore might not have certain extra finishing on the cover.

1

It was the last night of a very long vacation. School usually started in July, but we were now in the last week of August. For once, my bag was all packed. I had needed something to do, although reminding myself that school was beginning the next day hadn't done much for my mood. I looked glumly at my neatly ironed uniform. Partly because it was brand new so it was still all stiff and uncomfortable, partly because it was so ugly (yellow and brown for middle school) and partly because of everything that had happened over the summer.

My best friend Pallavi had left town three weeks ago, and an email from her had arrived almost immediately. We had promised each other we'd write every week. I had not kept up my side of the bargain yet. Her mail had sounded chirpy—it was all about her new hostel room, her roommate and the other people in her class.

I read it for what was probably the fifth time since it had arrived and made up my mind that I would write back once I had something to write about. The last two weeks had been fairly uneventful for me. My only accomplishments had been watching some really boring movies on TV and trying to feed the neighbourhood cat vegetables. If Pallavi had been here, both these activities would have led to at least a day of intense discussion, but on email it just didn't feel the same.

I closed the tab and looked up at my father, who was smiling at me over his book. My parents had spent all summer reading thick books with titles like *Flowers Learning to Bloom: Effective Education and the Role of Freedom*. This had begun in March.

There was a Parent-Teachers' Association meeting that month, in which everyone was told that the Trust which had been running the Hill School for Girls in Lailapaani for so many years had finally run out of money. The school had been turned over to a new group of people, who had lots of new-fangled ideas about how to run schools. The school would now be called 'The Hill School for Holistic Learning'. Whatever that means.

There was a big fight at the PTA meeting—I know this because Pallavi's mum said that she had 'no patience with flaky people who think they can tell everyone else how to raise their children' and said some very rude things about the others in the PTA.

My parents were also at this PTA meeting, but they refused to tell me much about it, because they said they didn't want to prejudice me against the new school. So Pallavi went away to a boarding school in the city, and I am still here, supposedly because my parents ordered some reading material online, written by the new principal, and made what my mother calls 'an informed choice'. I think it's because they're lazy and it's easier to read some books than to think about what is best for their only child. Thanks to all the restructuring, the school reopening had been postponed by almost six weeks, which meant all the other schools, including Pallavi's, reopened ages ago.

I stared back at my father, who was still smiling, though his smile was beginning to look forced. 'Are you going to write back to Pallavi?'

'Later,' I said.

'Things are going to be different this year without her, aren't they?'

'No, why should they be?' I asked sweetly. I had spent pretty much the entire vacation telling them that school would never be the same without Pallavi. They had spent the vacation trying to make me see the bright side of things, but their attempts had failed from the start.

He ignored my tone and powered through. 'You know, your new principal sounds really smart. She writes wonderfully. You should try and read some of this, you might enjoy it.'

You might enjoy it. I had been hearing that all summer, and it was beginning to get on my nerves.

'Or I might hate it,' I said.

'You're being rude again, Elizabeth,' my mother said, walking in. 'And you're not going to enjoy anything until you try. I hear there are going to be a lot of new kids in your class this year. It might be good to try and meet some new people.'

I wasn't very good at meeting new people, and my parents knew this. Pallavi and I had been pretty much inseparable for years and, while I got along with the other girls in my class in a remote sort of way, I didn't really have any other friends. I could see that my parents were still trying really hard to make the best of it, so I chose silence over the next nasty thing I was about to say.

I went to bed knowing I wasn't going to get any sleep that night, just like every other night that summer. I would wander around the house, read, or try to get food out of the fridge without waking anyone up. Earlier, sometimes I'd go stay at Pallavi's, but that started getting depressing because she was packing to leave and it reminded me of how awful everything was going to be.

2

The next day I went into the Class VII classroom, from where we were all immediately herded into the auditorium for an introduction to our new principal.

Her name was Palak Nanda, and I had seen her picture at the back of the books that had been lying around my house. She looked about as old as my parents, which is not very, compared to our previous principal, who was ancient and preferred to speak to us as little as possible.

She was standing on the stage with a bunch of teachers, some of whom I recognised, many of whom I didn't. I saw my maths teacher, Shabnam Miss, and waved, but she didn't see me. I sat down just as Palak Nanda began her speech.

'I would like to begin by telling you all how *very* happy and privileged it makes me feel to see your beautiful faces this morning. I know many things may have changed for you since last year—many of your teachers from the previous year have left, which is very sad, but they had a different *path*. I know some of you must be in a very *vulnerable space* right now,' she said, lowering her voice, 'and I would like a chance to *explore* those feelings with you. Above all, I want this school to be a space of *exploration*. Since the term has started almost six weeks late, we will not be having a long break at Diwali, as you all know. We will, instead, take a short three-day break. We have a lot of wonderful experiences ahead of us this term. There have been several changes made to your curriculum and schedules, and your teachers will guide you through these. We want to create the kind of learning that *you* want. The kind of school that *you* want.'

I had no idea what she was talking about so I looked around me, just in case there was someone who looked like they did. My classmate, Mahrukh, who was a day scholar like me, was sitting next to me and did not appear to be in a *vulnerable space*—she was irritating a centipede that was walking up her arm by poking it with a twig.

'That's mean,' I whispered.

'Shh. Principal's talking,' she said, without looking at me.

This really irritated me, so I looked around to see if there were any teachers around I could complain to, and decided that I was not that kind of person. I turned my attention back to the principal, who was, in fact, still talking. She was saying that people have different ways of exploring and seeing their world, and that all these ways were important and must be respected. I agreed completely, and made a mental note to use this argument with my parents who frequently made it their business to disrespect my way of seeing the world.

Just then, Palak Nanda announced that, because this was the case, all unit tests would be replaced by 'creative projects' that we *would not be given marks for*. A few of the older girls applauded, but I felt a hot flash of panic, which immediately turned cold as I realised why my parents had been so reluctant to send me to the school that Pallavi had gone to. *They thought I was stupid.*

I had always been the best at maths in my class, but not very good at anything else, and while I tried my best to come first every year, my parents always told me it was okay. Now I knew why.

Back in class, we had to arrange our desks in a circle and talk about ourselves and what we were looking forward to in the coming year. Tanveen Miss, who had been the Class VII class teacher for as long as anybody could remember, seemed unnecessarily excited about this.

'We're going to use today to get to know one another. Let *me* start,' she said and immediately began telling us about her dog, Bowbow, and her three children, whose names she didn't mention.

I took this time to reflect on how small our class had become—there used to be about thirty-five people and now there were only eighteen, about a third of whom were new kids. I tuned back in to find that Tanveen Miss seemed to have lost everybody's attention. 'I look forward to a year of learning and ... teaching. And *exploring*,' she added, looking pleased with herself.

A few people said that they were looking forward to making new friends. Mahrukh said pointedly that she was looking forward to using the basketball court again, since someone from this class whom she didn't want to name had broken the basket last year by hanging from it just to show off, and we all looked at Suchi, who said nothing.

When it was my turn, I said 'maths class', because it was really the only thing I was looking forward to. After that, everyone said 'history', 'science', 'English', or 'Sports Day', and we were done pretty quickly.

Tanveen Miss quickly announced that she had another activity planned for us, which made me a little nervous. She had taken a few classes for us before—she loved giving us activities, but they usually ended badly.

'Some of you know the school grounds well; for some of you, it's your first day. We have to learn to *embrace* our surroundings. Embrace your loved ones, your learning, your *world.* It's like Ms Nanda always says,' she said dreamily, 'to know, you have to *feel.* And today we are going to do exactly that. I want each of you to pick an object in the school grounds to connect with. Bond with it. Speak to it. Learn to care for it. Or simply learn to enjoy its silence. We'll meet back here in an hour.'

'Miss, can I choose a desk?' asked Rajni, who had been dozing on hers.

'No,' said Tanveen Miss.

'Miss, pencil!' shouted someone else.

'No!' Tanveen Miss was getting visibly upset. 'Outside. All of you, go *outside.*'

The questions continued, though, and Tanveen Miss finally announced that we were to each find a tree to connect with.

As we trailed out of the classroom, I saw Tanveen Miss smile, pull out a book and start reading. This suited me fine, and oddly made me like her a little more, since I was planning to do the same thing. The only thing was to make sure I got to the spot I had in mind before anybody else did.

It was a large tree with plenty of shade. If Tanveen Miss were to come check on us, I could pretend that I was talking to it. Also, the trunk was covered in thorns and was generally known to attract snakes, so I wouldn't be expected to go hugging it or anything. If this was the kind of thing we'd be expected to do from now on, I thought, it wouldn't be so bad.

Everyone ran off in different directions. I could see that Rajni had found a loophole and was lying horizontal on a stone bench (which had a small plant growing under it), and was hugging it with her eyes shut. I had assumed that most of the others would have gone off in their groups to play, but surprisingly, most people had followed Tanveen Miss's instructions and at the very least had found themselves something to sit near, or around, or on top of.

As I headed off towards my tree, I heard someone humming behind me and turned around. It was one of the new girls, who I think was a hostel girl. She smiled at me, and I smiled vaguely back and kept walking, quickening my pace a little. It wasn't that I didn't want to talk to her, I just didn't want her to see my tree and take it. Okay, I didn't much want to talk to her, either.

She seemed to be following me though, so I walked a little faster and settled down quickly under my tree. I pulled Pallavi's email out of my skirt pocket and read through it again—I'd printed it out so I could read it without my parents looking over my shoulder. She said that she was missing home terribly and that none of her classmates were much fun and so on, but at least she sounded busy.

I was incredibly jealous of her for that. I was sitting under a tree.

In about ten minutes, I was sleepy and began to get that slightly panicky feeling you get when you're exhausted and can't do anything about it. I couldn't lean back because of the thorns and I couldn't lie down because of the snakes, so I muttered to myself, 'I'mtired I'mtired I'mtired I'mtired', which I do sometimes when I'm restless and don't know what to do.

'Are you talking to yourself?' said a voice a little further away. It was the new girl who had followed me. She had found herself a big rock and climbed on top of it.

'No, I'm talking to the tree,' I said quickly.

'That's all right then, I guess,' she said, frowning slightly. 'That's what you're supposed to do. At least you two are getting along. Mine's giving me the silent treatment.'

I looked at the tree she'd chosen. It was one we used to climb when we were little. The rock next to it gave us a leg up. We loved it, but it was struck by lightning once and now it had no leaves and the branches were charred and unstable. 'Maybe because it's dead,' I told her.

'It's undead. A zombie tree,' she said, affectionately rubbing her hand against the crumbling bark. 'Have you ever seen a zombie?'

'Of course not!'

'Neither have I,' she said sadly. 'You're Elizabeth, right? I'm Ayesha.'

Ayesha didn't say anything after that, so I pulled out my notebook to write out a draft of my reply to Pallavi's letter. I had gotten as far as 'Dear Pallavi' when Ayesha piped up again.

'I think I need to sing to it.'

'So sing to it.'

'I was *joking. God.* Do I look like the sort of person who would sing to a tree?'

I told her I had no idea what kind of person she looked like, and anyway, I had read somewhere that playing music to plants helped them grow.

'Although,' I pointed out calmly, 'this might not work in your case since you were stupid enough to choose a tree that's already dead.'

'You're really rude, you know? I was only trying to make conversation. What kind of school makes you do this stuff, anyway?'

This was the question I had been asking myself as well, and I had to admit I didn't have the answer. I also knew that I had been rude to Ayesha, and thought vaguely that I should be trying to make friends now that I didn't have any.

Suddenly, I wasn't in the mood to compose that mail anymore. I pushed my notebook back into my bag.

Ayesha stood up in a huff, jumped off the rock she was on and began to stomp off, then turned around quickly when she saw Tanveen Miss walking towards us.

'How's it going, girls?' she asked cheerfully.

I wasn't sure what the appropriate answer to that was, so I hugged my knees and smiled.

Ayesha complained, 'Miss, she's distracting me! And she said my tree was stupid because it's dead!'

'Everything is deserving of respect,' said Tanveen Miss, looking up at it doubtfully.

'I think she should apologise to it,' said Ayesha, smugly.

Instantly, I hated her. I glared at Ayesha, ready for a fight if it came to that.

'No need for that,' Tanveen Miss mumbled, looking at me warily. 'Anyway. Looks like it's going well.' She disappeared.

I was very glad when the bell rang half an hour later for class to be over.

On my way back to class, I saw Mahrukh hanging off the branch of a mango tree, shouting, 'Miss, nothing's happening!'

Two girls had gotten into a fight over a tree they'd both wanted, and had spent the entire period arguing and crying.

Poor Tanveen Miss was looking miserable.

I didn't get much sleep that night either. When this started in the summer, I had pleaded with my parents to be allowed to move the TV out of their bedroom, so that I had something to keep myself occupied with and fall asleep to. It was taken back in a couple of days when I was found lying asleep in front of something on TV which I should have been under no circumstances allowed to watch, in my mother's words. So that was that.

With nothing else to entertain me, I wandered over to the fridge to see if there was anything there that might interest me. We had had my favourite food for dinner, so I was hopeful.

A few minutes later, I had piled some rice and fish curry onto my plate and was sitting on my bed happily. Since I had no plans after that, I wandered around the house for a while. I picked up Palak Nanda's book from a table that it had been lying on for a few days and opened it. I noticed that she wrote exactly like she spoke. Tanveen Miss had begun to speak that way as well. I had told my mother, the most sensible person I knew, about what we had had to do that day.

'Trees? Really?' she had asked, incredulously.

'Yes, can you imagine? It was really weird. I'm telling you,' I said grimly, 'this was a bad idea.'

'I don't know, you might enjoy it.'

There it was again.

'I sometimes wish they'd let the kids at my school have a little fun. They're always studying, poor things. No time at all for anything else.'

My mother worked at the office of the Baldwin Boys' School. I was surprised to hear her say this, because her constant complaint was usually that our school didn't take studies as seriously as they did. She was the last person I would've expected to be happy about this new development, but I could tell she was trying to be positive about the whole thing. I did not want someone to help me be positive about things.

I went to my parents' bedroom to see if my father would be of use. He was always complaining about the state of the world, so I figured he could be counted on to be on my side.

As soon as I started my story about the day, though, I realised how wrong I was. My father is a Forest Officer, so when he heard that we had spent an entire class watching trees, he was thrilled. He immediately turned off the Malayalam movie he was watching and started asking me questions.

'What kind of tree?'

'I don't know. Thorny. Big. Anyway, so we had to *talk* ...'

'You should ask. Always ask. When I was your age, I had a big book full of the household names and scientific names of plants. I can find it for you ...' he pulled out a trunk from under the bed and started looking through it. He was always trying to get me more interested in nature. We had tried fishing, birdwatching, gardening and hiking, but nothing had ever stuck.

'It's got to be around here somewhere,' he said, looking confused.

'That's fine. You can give it to me later,' I assured him hurriedly. I had to listen to him talk for a bit about how we live amidst great beauty and how glad he was that someone was taking the trouble to teach us kids how to observe and appreciate the world around us.

Clearly, I was not going to be able to enlist the support of my parents. I was also not going to be able to read Palak Nanda's book, because I couldn't understand a word of it.

I pulled out another book from the shelf and took it with me to bed. It was called *How To Be An Assertive Woman*. My mother had found it at a secondhand bookstore in town and given it to my father as a present.

She had found this hilarious.

I read the entire thing before I finally fell asleep.

3

I had started walking to school with a girl called Rakshita. This was initially because she was my mum's colleague's daughter, who lived next door, and had just transferred to my class at school from wherever she had been before. Where exactly was unclear to me, because Rakshita talked extremely fast. It sometimes made conversations a bit awkward.

'Sowhatyoubroughtforlunch?' she asked me that morning.

'What?'

'Whatyoubroughtforlunch?'

'Say that again.'

'What.You.Brought.For.Lunch.'

'Rotis.'

'Oh.'

We walked a little while in silence. Then she said, 'Ido n'tknowaboutyoubutIdidn'treallylikethewaythatgirlspoke atassemblyyouknowtheonewiththefunnyponytail.

‘Ah,’ I told her, not even trying. Normally, I at least tried to understand what she was saying, but that morning I wasn’t in the mood.

We had a new teacher teaching us social studies. I had never been particularly good at either history or geography, but the sight of this woman every morning made me sure that neither of these subjects would ever hold any appeal for me.

If Palak Nanda’s schemes had made Tanveen Miss a more cheerful, if slightly more annoying, person, it had obviously not had the same effect on Indu Miss. She had an air of disapproval about her, which made me extremely nervous in her class. This wouldn’t have been a problem except that our evaluation in social studies this year was to be on the basis of presentations, instead of exams.

On her first day, Indu Miss denounced the examination system and told us that in her class, no one would get away with mugging up answers to question papers. Since there was nothing she could do about the fact that she would have to assess all of us at the end of the year, she would be trying out other ways to test us.

‘I know most of you have been very well trained,’ she had said nastily, ‘in learning *facts*. This will be useless to you here. Our evaluation techniques this year will attempt to be more holistic, and will hopefully inculcate the ability to *think*.’

I should have been glad. Learning names and dates by heart was a constant source of misery for me. That was why I liked maths so much better—once you understood what you had to do to solve one sum, you could figure out the rest on your own.

The odd thing was that when Tanveen Miss or even Palak Nanda talked about our education being 'holistic' (which I eventually had to look up in the dictionary), it sounded happy and fun, or at the very least what they thought was fun, which included talking to trees and telling everyone how we felt all the time. When Indu Miss said it, it sounded like a threat. Her way of making us *think* was to get each of us to do a presentation for fifteen minutes in front of the entire class.

I had to do a presentation on the history of paper. I had been hoping that my turn would come towards the end. For a while, it seemed like it would, because there were a lot of people who were desperate to do their presentations. There are a lot of girls like that in my class.

I had spent the previous night writing out my essay. I practised once in front of a mirror (my mother's advice), which didn't work at all because I kept thinking how silly I looked. When I got too nervous to work anymore, I made a list of things to do that would make me feel better. I referred once or twice to *How To Be an Assertive Woman*, which had a section on 'How To Present Yourself: Look Successful To Be Successful'. I had to skip the parts on how to dress—I wasn't allowed to wear high heels and I wasn't sure what a 'power suit' was.

In class that day, my stomach began to hurt. I had only spoken in public twice in my life, and both times were disasters. The first time was when I was six, and my parents had made me go to a poetry recitation competition. They told me it was just for fun, and there was no reason to be nervous. And I didn't even know that I would be, because I'd never done anything like it before. When I got on stage to read my poem, I looked out at all those people and froze. Two whole minutes of silence later, my mother had had to lead me off the stage.

The second time was just as bad. I had a talking part in one of the Annual Day plays. My legs began to shake and I went straight to the end of my dialogue, completely skipping a bit where one of the other girls had to speak. It was her only line in the play, so she was furious.

I was fine when I started the presentation. I began to read out the essay, which even I had to admit was pretty good. I had just gotten past the first paragraph when Indu Miss interrupted me.

'I don't want you reading it out, Elizabeth.'

'Sorry, miss. What, miss?' I asked incoherently.

'I said I don't want you to read it out. Speak to the class.'

Luckily, I remembered most of it, so I fixed my eyes on one of the cupboards lining the walls and started talking. I noticed vaguely that a couple of people were smiling at me, but I couldn't figure out whether they were encouraging smiles or smirks. Again, I was only a few sentences in before Indu Miss started up again.

'Explain what you just said,' she told me. She looked unfriendly.

'Miss?'

'It sounds like you've just memorised everything. Did you even write the presentation yourself? I am looking for *understanding*. Not *mugging*.'

I remembered the part in *How To Be An Assertive Woman* on how to deal with criticism. Respond calmly and with authority, I told myself. I tried to stop my hands from shaking uncontrollably and failed.

'Explain it to me casually, like you would to a friend,' she said, more kindly.

Suddenly I felt hot anger towards her. To my horror, instead of launching into a calm and authoritative answer to her question, I felt my head get woozy and my eyes well up with tears.

'I don't know,' I said, even though I did.

'That's what I thought,' she said.

She sat there smugly while I read out the rest of my presentation rapidly. When I finally went back to my seat, I saw one of the new girls smile at me and roll her eyes at Indu Miss. I looked away.

The next morning, Rakshita was being nicer to me and, while she tactfully avoided the subject of the previous day's class, I suspected that was the reason. I was beginning to wonder how things could get any worse than they already were, but I was sure that they somehow would.

Our desks were now arranged in a circle around the classroom and, to my irritation, Ayesha's seat was right across from mine. She had made a friend—the girl who had smiled at me in Indu Miss's class. Her name was Maitreyi, and like most of the new girls, she was also a hostel girl. They sat next to each other in class. My desk partner was Rakshita, who didn't know anyone but me when school had started, but had now begun to hang around with Rajni and a couple of other people.

Tanveen Miss walked in and announced that she had an

activity for us. Some people groaned, and one voice said 'Noooo ...'

She pretended not to notice, started handing out sheets of paper and told us to choose partners. Rakshita looked at me nervously.

'So ... Whoyougonnachoose?'

'Oh, one of my friends,' I said, untruthfully.

'Iamgoingtogooverthereokay?' she said, relieved, and moved across the room to try and wake Rajni up.

I saw Mahrukh at her desk and decided to go over and sit next to her. She was one of the very few other people in the class who hadn't immediately picked a partner.

I had always been a little wary of Mahrukh. She was one of those people who seemed to enjoy being by herself, and never seemed to prefer anyone's company over anyone else's. Many of the girls in class wanted to hang out with her, but she would eventually go off by herself.

'Want to be partners?' I asked casually.

'Sure,' she said, and like that, it was done.

Tanveen Miss passed around maps of our town along with worksheets. The questions on the worksheets were easy—we had to write down the location of various places in town by looking at the map. Tanveen Miss suggested that people from out of town team up with those who were from here, but since everyone had chosen their partners, no one wanted to change.

'Let's start with the easy ones,' I said. 'Central Market.'

Mahrukh marked it on the map, along with the Lailapaani

Public Library, which was question two. Soon we were on a roll, guessing locations without even looking at the map. We were done in no time.

'Let's put places that aren't in the questions,' suggested Mahrukh.

'Like what?'

'Like this one,' she said, circling a spot in the woods. 'Really good for climbing rocks. I think that's where it is. Your turn.' She handed me the pencil.

'I'm not really allowed to go around there by myself,' I told her.

'Oh, me neither. I used to go with my older sister before she went off to college. I haven't been there in a while.'

The hour passed easily. At the end of the class, Tanveen Miss announced the second part of the activity. Our project for the term would be to go around town in groups and collect information on a particular area, or a particular topic. This was to encourage us to know our surroundings a little better.

Tanveen Miss's class was the last of the day, and Mahrukh decided to walk home from school with Rakshita and me. I noticed immediately that having her around made the conversation a lot less stressful. Rakshita really liked Mahrukh and I felt pleased to have been the one who brought her along. We complained good-naturedly about Tanveen Miss and a little less good-naturedly about Indu Miss.

'She probably hates me now,' I said, gloomily.

'I don't think she likes anyone,' said Mahrukh. 'I don't

think she likes kids. She's the warden, so imagine how bad the hostel kids have it. She came to the shop once when I was there.'

'Whatdidshebuy?' asked Rakshita, in wonder.

'A toothbrush. And a sewing kit. She was sitting there waiting for the bill and I told her to wait because my father was in the storeroom at the back. She asked me if they taught me basic addition in school.'

'What did you say?'

'I said miss, I'm in your school. Then she said, "Oh, no wonder."'

This made us giggle. We reached Mahrukh's house. Her parents ran Empire Stores, which was a bakery and also a sort of general store, and it was on the way from the school to my house. Mahrukh was about to go in when she said, 'So I guess we'll be in the same group tomorrow?'

'I guess so,' I told her, trying not to look too pleased.

I'd had another completely sleepless night and my parents found it impossible to wake me up the next morning. They were getting late too, so there was yelling, and they finally gave up and went to work. I woke up in a panic and decided to go to class anyway—I had social studies that day, and I didn't want to get yelled at by Indu Miss for skipping class, on top of everything else.

When I finally got to school, I had already missed assembly. I was hoping I wouldn't run into any teachers on the way—I was not good at making up lies, and certainly not under pressure. This hope, like all my hopes, was dashed, in the worst way possible. Indu Miss and Palak Nanda were standing right in my way.

'Good morning miss,' I said, trying a sheepish-but-friendly smile. Indu Miss turned on me instantly.

'Are you just walking in? Is this honestly the kind of behaviour we're supposed to deal with?'

'No miss,' I said, automatically. I was going to be punished for sure. I hoped against hope that it would be getting sent home and not standing outside class—people stared, and it looked like it was going to rain.

'So you don't think you need to come for the morning assembly, is that it?'

'I need to, miss.'

'Palak, this is exactly the attitude I was talking about. No respect for learning. Just get your marks and go. You deal with this,' she said, exasperatedly.

Palak Nanda looked nervous. 'Maybe she has a reason. A legitimate reason?' she looked at me hopefully.

'You don't look sick,' Indu Miss decided. 'Are you sick?'

'No, miss.'

'Then why?'

Pallavi had once told me that when I wanted to lie, it was best to stay as close as possible to the truth. She had read it in a book. She was very good at lying. They were both looking at me expectantly, so I panicked and blurted out the truth instead. Indu Miss was furious.

'You didn't wake up on time?! Look at that, Palak. She doesn't even care enough to lie!' she said, which confused me.

'Yes, intolerable,' said Palak, looking genuinely upset. 'Very intolerable. Not very nice at all. Assembly was just wonderful today. They read out the news and Tanveen Miss showed us how to cross-stitch. Very interesting.'

I tried to look as if this made me sad. Indu Miss saw right through me and suggested that I be sent home and not be allowed to saunter in whenever I liked. Palak Nanda was against this course of action and seemed to think that my having skipped such a lovely assembly was punishment enough. There was a brief negotiation and it was decided that I would have to write a 500-word essay on 'Respect for Learning'.

'Which will be handed over to me,' said Indu Miss, sharply. Palak Nanda did not argue, clearly glad to be rid of me.

I was even later for first period, which was Tanveen Miss's class. Thankfully, she didn't notice me entering. I looked around for Mahrukh, and was dismayed when I saw who she was sitting with.

Mahrukh and Maitreyi were discussing their maps, and Ayesha was looking right at me. I looked around for a moment, wondering what I had missed.

Tanveen Miss came over towards me. Before she had a chance to scold me, I said, 'Sorry miss, I was late for assembly and then I was talking to Indu Miss outside.'

'Oh, that's all right,' she said, 'but do you know what group you're in?'

Suddenly Mahrukh piped up from her seat. 'Elizabeth, over here! Miss, she's in my group!'

I realised, heart sinking, that, thanks to the fact that I had been late by only ten minutes, groups had already been chosen for the term project and this would be mine for the next few months. I went over to them.

'Where were you?' Ayesha demanded.

'None of your business,' I shot back.

'Is she always like this?' she asked Mahrukh, who shrugged.

I really didn't want to be the cranky one in the group, so I let the others fill me in on what had happened so far. Everyone had been given one aspect to focus on, and ours was food. We were supposed to do our project on food habits in the city. I liked the idea—Maitreyi had suggested it, and it sounded pretty fun. There were families from all over the place living in Lailapaani, and there were many different kinds of food that they ate.

Predictably, there was resistance.

'Why food?! So boooring, yaar,' said Ayesha. No one said anything. 'Why not something fun? Like music?' she persisted.

'This is our annual project,' I told her calmly. 'It's not supposed to be fun. It's supposed to be good.'

'I think it's fun,' said Maitreyi.

'You think everything is fun,' Ayesha said, sulkily. I had gathered that Ayesha and Maitreyi, in addition to sitting on adjacent desks, were also roommates in the hostel. Ayesha eventually stopped complaining and settled into a sulk, which worked fine for everyone.

'We're supposed to find out about the food habits of people in the town and do a project on it, miss said. We can do it any way we want,' said Maitreyi.

'We could start by asking people,' suggested Ayesha, who had come out of her sulk.

'Sounds good. I can talk to the customers who come to buy food at my parents' shop,' said Mahrukh.

'Can I come?' asked Maitreyi.

'Yeah. Elizabeth can talk to a few people in her neighbourhood, to start with.'

'What about me?' asked Ayesha.

'You can interview people in the hostel,' I told her, firmly. I wanted to avoid spending all my evenings with Ayesha.

'I know what we should do,' said Maitreyi suddenly. 'We should have a party, and get people to bring food. That could be our project.'

We looked at her sceptically.

'Miss said we could do anything,' said Mahrukh, tentatively.

'We are getting graded on this, right?' I asked. 'Because if we're not, then let's have a party.'

Maitreyi looked disappointed. Ayesha said, 'Oh, don't worry, Elizabeth. We'll do your boring project. You'll get your grades.'

'I'm only saying ...' I started, but Maitreyi cut me off.

'Never mind. We'll start tomorrow, okay?'

I was relieved when it was time for our next class, which was maths. I liked my teacher, Shabnam Miss, and she had always liked me. I had never had any trouble with maths and, because I was one of the few people in class who didn't find it boring, she and I had always gotten along fine. Sometimes Shabnam Miss would give me extra sums for my homework. I had told Pallavi about this once and she made fun of me for being a goody two shoes. I had gotten really upset and we had had a fight. We made up eventually, though. That day, Shabnam Miss gave me a worksheet full of puzzles, and I was able to go home looking forward to something.

5

I was walking around my neighbourhood, feeling very pleased with myself for having suggested that I do this part of the project on my own. I had started by speaking to three families in my area, which was full of Malayalis. One would have thought this was the easy way out, but it wasn't—everyone I spoke to knew me and my parents, so I had to endure several cups of tea and questions about school and my family.

Ayesha was hopefully doing what she was supposed to do in the hostel, and Mahrukh and Maitreyi were asking people who came to Empire Stores. Hostel girls were only allowed into town on weekends, but Maitreyi had got special permission from Tanveen Miss.

The four of us had decided to meet on Saturday at Mahrukh's parents' shop to figure out what to do next. Mahrukh and Maitreyi were inside, eating chips. I said hello to Mahrukh's dad and went over to them.

'We're still waiting for Ayesha,' said Maitreyi. 'She's at the hostel. She'll be here soon. She was waiting for a phone call from home.'

‘Cool. So what’re we planning to do today?’ I asked.

‘I was just telling Maitreyi about this place I once went to,’ Mahrukh said. ‘In the woods. We should go there.’

‘Let’s go there now!’ said Maitreyi, excitedly. ‘Mahrukh says we can climb rocks and stuff. And there’s a stream.’

‘We should probably discuss the project, since we’re all here. We can go to the woods anytime,’ I told them.

‘The two of you can,’ Maitreyi pointed out. ‘I can’t go to the woods anytime. We’re not allowed to go anywhere alone without permission. Even during Thinking Time, we’re only allowed to go as far as the school compound.’

I didn’t ask, but Mahrukh did. One of us had to. ‘Thinking Time?’

‘Yeah. It’s time to Think. All the hostel kids have to do it. We can sit anywhere we like and do it. Then we have to say what we thought about.’

That didn’t sound acceptable to me at all. I wouldn’t want to tell people what I thought about when I was by myself. Everybody would hate me. I wondered if Pallavi was doing stuff like this in the hostel she was in, but then I remembered that she was sent there so that she wouldn’t have to.

‘What do you have to think about?’ asked Mahrukh.

‘I don’t know, anything. Last week I thought about insects. Not about insects generally, just how there are so many of them and how it must feel to be an insect. There were a lot of mosquitoes that day, so that’s probably why I thought about them so much.’

‘That’s really weird,’ said Mahrukh, peering at Maitreyi with concern.

'No, it's okay. I don't mind so much, we used to have to talk a lot at my old school.'

I felt really bad for Maitreyi. I figured she deserved to do something fun for a change.

'Okay, let's go. We can talk about the project there,' I said.

We decided to go pick up Ayesha from the hostel, because it was on our way. Maitreyi went upstairs to get her. When they came back, Ayesha was looking cheerful.

'Finally, a fun idea!' she said. 'I was beginning to think I'd be bored forever.'

The place Mahrukh took us to was beautiful. We had to walk a bit through the woods until we reached a small stream. From there, we had to climb up a bunch of rocks and then down again until we reached a clearing and a small cliff. Our town wasn't a big one, but it was near a large hill station. There were always a few tourists hanging around, and there weren't many places you could go that were totally isolated. That day, the walk downhill was very slippery, because it had been raining a bit the past few days.

'Are we allowed to be here?' I asked Mahrukh.

'You mean, is it against the law? I don't think so,' she replied.

'She means do your parents know,' said Ayesha.

'They know I used to come here with my sister sometimes. It's safe, though. My sister used to come here with her friends all the time.'

When we reached the spot, Maitreyi squealed with joy and immediately scrambled up one of the high rocks. I followed her halfway and settled into a nook that didn't look too scary.

'I used to do this at my old school,' said Maitreyi. 'It was really pretty. Not as pretty as here, because it wasn't so hilly, but we used to be able to go out a lot more.'

'Maitreyi's old school was even more mental than this one,' said Ayesha, rolling her eyes.

'More mental than Thinking Time?' asked Mahrukh, laughing.

'Much more,' said Maitreyi delightedly. 'No tests even. And we didn't have to sit in the classroom if we didn't want to.'

No wonder she seemed so calm about everything here, I thought. 'Where did you sit, then?' I asked her.

'Outside, mostly,' she said. 'Wherever we felt like.'

'That sounds awesome,' said Mahrukh wistfully.

'We had classrooms,' said Ayesha. 'In my school in Delhi. Really nice ones. And we didn't have to do anything ridiculous.'

'So why did you leave?' asked Mahrukh.

Ayesha glanced at Maitreyi, who smiled.

'I didn't want to leave. I had loads of friends. I hate this stupid place,' she said, jumping off the tree branch she was sitting on.

I could feel myself getting irritated again. 'So go back,' I told her.

'I wish! My stupid parents won't let me. I ask them every time they call, and they always say no.'

'So stop complaining,' I snapped at her.

'You're one to talk,' she snapped back. 'You're the one

who's always complaining about everything. "Oh, it's so dangerous to come here. Oh, the tree is dead."'

'IT WAS DEAD!' I shouted.

Ayesha lost her temper. 'Who wants to do all this anyway? This place is so boring, no wonder you're so cranky all the time! There isn't even anything to do here. I can't believe your idea of fun is to come to some stupid forest.'

'You said you wanted to come here, didn't you? And why are you here anyway? Did they throw you out of Delhi or something?'

Maitreyi burst out laughing and quickly stopped when she caught Ayesha glaring at her furiously.

'Seriously?' I asked amazed. 'They threw you out of Delhi?'

'Not out of Delhi, obviously. Out of her school. Sorry!' Maitreyi said to Ayesha, who was shaking with anger. 'I didn't mean to laugh, I didn't think it was that big a deal.'

'I told you that as a secret!' yelled Ayesha.

'You should have said so then!' said Maitreyi. 'Why is it such a big secret anyway? You know,' she said, looking at me and Mahrukh, 'she won't even tell me why they threw her out. I asked her and asked her. But she won't tell anyone.'

'Will you stop telling them things!'

'I don't know why you're so dramatic all the time. Things are only a big deal if you make them a big deal,' said Maitreyi, so primly that even I got irritated.

'Oh yeah? Is that what Indu Miss says to you? No wonder you're such a goody-goody, with a mother like that,' said Ayesha.

'Indu Miss is your mother?' I asked, incredulously.

'Yes, she is! And the only reason I know is because we're in the same hostel room. Otherwise she doesn't tell people, do you, Maitreyi?' asked Ayesha.

'It's nobody's business, okay?' said Maitreyi, beginning to get angry.

'No wonder you never get into trouble in her class!' I shouted.

'That's not true!' said Maitreyi, sounding really upset.

'Whatever,' said Ayesha. 'And you're really one to talk, Elizabeth. Always going on about grades. You're so boring. And rude. No wonder you're always by yourself.'

That hurt. I yelled back, 'And no wonder you got thrown out of Delhi! I hope they throw you out of here next!'

'You're both horrible! I can't believe I have to do this project with you!' screamed Maitreyi, who had finally and totally lost her temper.

'Teacher's pet!'

'Snob!'

'Bore!'

Maitreyi, Ayesha and I were glaring at each other angrily, with nothing left to say. That's when we realised that Mahrukh was gone.

6

Since Mahrukh had led us into the woods so confidently, none of us had really bothered to see where we were going. We had no idea how to get out, and it had started drizzling. We were all too mad at each other to talk much, but we were too scared to walk separately. Ayesha was trying the hardest to be brave, or at least to pretend.

'I think this is the way we came,' she said, pointing to a hopelessly slippery-looking path. Maitreyi shrugged.

'You two could at least try to help,' snapped Ayesha. 'Unless you want to live here forever.'

I didn't say anything because I was busy fighting back tears.

Maitreyi glowered. 'Fine, let's go that way. As if any of us know, anyway. I can't believe Mahrukh would do this to us,' she said.

'Why wouldn't she? I'd have left you here myself, if I'd had any idea how to get back,' said Ayesha cruelly.

'Just stop talking,' snarled Maitreyi, sounding so furious

that Ayesha shut up immediately, though she still tried to look like she didn't care.

I was sick of listening to their bickering so I walked ahead, even though I was terrified. It was beginning to rain harder, and we all had to walk carefully, because we were trying not to slip in the mud. I fell down twice and Maitreyi and Ayesha fell down once each, but no one was even in the mood to laugh at anyone else. We were wet, filthy and exhausted.

Suddenly Maitreyi shouted, 'The road! I can see it, it's right ahead!'

We all hurried towards it, as quickly as we could with our jeans and shoes full of mud. There was a sudden sense of relief as we all realised we weren't going to die in the forest, but it wasn't nearly enough to lighten the mood between us.

As soon as we reached the point where the road led to the school and hostel, I walked off towards home without saying goodbye and neither of the others even looked up. I felt thankful that I was at least going home alone—Maitreyi and Ayesha were heading back to the same room in sullen silence, and I did not envy them that.

Back home, my parents had just begun to get worried. It was almost dark, and I didn't usually stay out that long. When they saw me, they knew immediately that I had been in the woods.

'I thought you were going out to do your project!' my mother yelled. 'Why would you lie to us?'

I burst into tears. I couldn't believe my awful luck. I was the one who hadn't wanted to go, I had almost died and now I was the one being yelled at. It was all horribly unfair.

I went to my room and slammed the door. My mother

followed me in. I think she felt bad, so she just told me to go take a bath, which I did. It made me feel slightly better, but not much, so I went out to make myself a cup of hot tea. My mother was waiting for me in the kitchen.

'What happened?' she asked.

'I don't want to talk about it,' I sniffled.

'Pallavi called while you were out. She said she would call back before dinnertime.'

'I don't want to talk to her today,' I said.

'That's not fair. She was asking if you were all right. She says you haven't replied to any of her emails. Just speak to her.'

Pallavi had sent me another mail. I didn't know why I hadn't written back. I guess I just didn't have anything to say, although I also knew that it was because I didn't want her to know that things weren't going so well here. The longer I put off writing to her, the harder it became. I hoped that she wouldn't call back, but at the same time, I was desperate to talk. This confused me and I felt even more miserable.

She did call, though. The phone rang while I was eating dinner, which I had taken into my room and was eating in bed. My parents had briefly objected to this, but had realised it wasn't worth the argument and settled down with their plates in front of the TV instead.

'Elizabeth, it's Pallavi!' my father shouted.

'Coming!' I shouted back, heart sinking. To refuse to talk to her right then would have caused too much of a scene, so I took my time getting out of bed. When I went outside, my father was chatting with Pallavi on the phone, asking about her parents and so on.

'Where have you been?' she snapped into the phone as soon as I picked it up, but she didn't sound angry.

'Here only,' I mumbled guiltily.

'"Here only,"' she imitated me, teasing. 'You haven't written back, and your father told me you've been in the woods. You've forgotten all about me, I knew you would. You have new friends now.'

I wanted to tell her I didn't, and I wanted to tell her what a horrible day I was having, but something about her cheerful tone made me decide not to. Instead, I asked, 'When are you coming back?'

'I don't know,' she said. 'We have a family get-together in Baroda for the Diwali holidays, so I'm going directly from here. I was going to come around Christmas, but there's also going to be a school trip during the vacation. It's optional, so I have to decide. Give me some news! What have you been doing?'

'Nothing,' I said. 'Nothing, nothing, nothing.'

'Are you all right?'

'Yes. My mother's calling me.' From across the room my mother stared at me, confused.

'Okay,' she said, sounding disappointed. She went quiet for a moment, and so did I.

'I'll write to you,' I said quickly, and put down the phone.

I went back to my room and did puzzles for about an hour before giving up. I got into bed after that, shut my eyes very tightly, and tried to sleep.

7

Luckily for us, all classes at school were cancelled for the next few days. Palak Nanda had organised a large conference for which she had invited people from different schools to talk about their ideas on education. She had held a special assembly for all of us to discuss this. She was very excited and kept flapping her hands around.

'I want this to be an opportunity for learning,' she told us. 'As teachers we have so much to learn.' Tanveen Miss nodded vigorously in the first row.

'We don't want to leave the students out of this wonderful opportunity, either,' she continued. 'I believe very strongly in your involvement at every stage. Your teachers will be too busy with the conference to take your regular classes. But don't worry!' she said, beaming, completely misunderstanding the hopeful expressions around her. 'There's plenty of work to go around, and many exciting activities are being planned for you all.'

So there were no classes, and we were still in school. Besides, Palak Nanda's idea of what counted as 'exciting activities' made me think that she was even madder than Tanveen Miss. Still, I was a little relieved, because it gave me some time before we had to figure out what to do about the project, which was very clearly not going anywhere after what had happened the previous day.

The teachers soon realised that getting us all to do things outside the classroom was even harder than taking classes. We were all given things to do, and Palak Nanda had generously offered us the option of sitting in on some of the sessions. Unfortunately, the teachers soon found many students using the sessions to take a nap or to avoid the 'activities' they didn't like. Following the morning session, all these students were discreetly but unceremoniously turned out of the hall and put back to work.

I had volunteered for kitchen duty, because Shabnam Miss was in charge. It was one of the least sought after jobs. There were lots of people fighting over the more glamorous work of showing the participants around the school, or cleaning and decorating the classrooms to 'make them look like human beings study in them,' as Indu Miss put it.

Kitchen duty meant having to serve tea and snacks to the people who had come to the conference, cleaning up a little in the kitchen and setting tables for lunch. The hostel mess was reserved for the conference people and only the students doing kitchen duty were allowed to eat at the mess that day.

I had also chosen kitchen duty because I knew Ayesha and Maitreyi wouldn't. Almost everyone who volunteered for kitchen duty was a day scholar. And I couldn't see Mahrukh anywhere, so she had obviously signed up for something else.

All the students doing kitchen duty were initially given a separate table, until Palak Nanda had a chat with Mary Miss, who was the cook-cum-kitchen supervisor at the hostel. After that, we were asked to spread out and sit at various tables so that we could interact with the conference participants. It made me nervous, so at lunchtime, I followed Rakshita.

'Why are you walking behind me like that?' she asked, so startled that she spoke slowly.

'Sorry,' I mumbled. 'Can I sit with you?'

'Come,' she said kindly. Rakshita and I had been getting along a lot better since Mahrukh had begun joining us on our walks from school.

Lunch was quite bad. To make it special, they had decided to serve puris that day, except that these puris were horrible and rubbery and oily. I avoided them completely and chose to eat everything else, which was completely lacking in oil and taste.

I was about to say something about the food when a lady who was sitting at the same table with us exclaimed, 'How rare to eat such wholesome food! Don't you think?' and turned to us. I noticed she hadn't taken any puris either so I guessed 'wholesome' meant 'without oil and salt'. I smiled at her and nodded, because I couldn't think of anything else to do.

'It has generally been a wonderful day,' she declared to Rakshita and me. Some other people around the table agreed noisily. 'But I am dying to know *your* opinion, that is, the children who are the recipients of this wonderful holistic education.' She smiled at us.

'I tried to go to one of the sessions,' I told her. 'But I didn't understand.' It was true, I did go to one. It was on "Introducing Technology Into the Learning Process and How Everybody Feels About It", or something like that; I didn't remember the name.

'Ho ho! Not surprising,' said a bald young man sitting across from me.

'No, I mean, what do you think of the new school? About Dr Nanda's plans?' asked the lady.

I stayed quiet, not knowing how to answer. Rakshita, on the hand, took the question very seriously. She drew a deep breath and began to rattle off a long list of complaints, rapidly. 'And look, eventhefoodissobad, in my last school atleastwhenpeoplecametheygaveusnonveg!' she ended, with satisfaction. Everyone at the table was gaping at her.

'We should go,' I told her hurriedly. I had finished my food. We said goodbye.

'*Wasted,*' I could hear the bald young man say as we left, 'on children ...'

Apart from working and organising, Palak Nanda had planned things to keep us busy. There were special classes and workshops in addition to everything we already had to do.

After lunch, I was ushered, without being asked, into a dance-yoga class. The man teaching it was from one of the schools that had been invited to the conference. Palak Nanda had begged him to take a class for some of our school's students and if he was happy to do it, it didn't show. He was very thin, had a long face and spoke in a soft drawl. He didn't seem like he was capable of anything as energetic as dancing.

'Dance-yoga is about combining the joy of dancing with the cleansing energy of yoga,' he told us sadly. 'It's about learning how to express what is inside you in a beautiful, creative way. You know?' he looked at us, heaving a big sigh.

'Yes, sir,' we chorused.

We were shuffled into our positions and made to sit down so we could begin, and I found myself sitting right next to Maitreyi. I tried to ignore her, which was easy for a while because the sad man had asked us to close our eyes and breathe. Next, he asked us to wave our hands around in the air with our eyes still shut.

'Feel free!' he breathed, slightly louder. 'No one can see you! Use your hands fully, send them into the sky!'

I opened my eyes slightly and noticed that the girl sitting in front of me was using her hands to tickle her friend sitting next to her, who was giggling. Someone else had smacked the people on either side of her and was whispering, 'Sorry, sorry.' The sad man hadn't noticed any of this and was waving his hands over his head frantically.

Maitreyi had opened her eyes as well, and had stopped doing the waving. 'This is the worst dance-yoga I've ever seen,' she said, to no one in particular.

I wanted to ask her what other kinds of dance-yoga she had seen, but then I remembered that I wasn't talking to her. I stopped waving my hands around as well, because I realised how silly everyone else was looking. And then, because it felt weird to just be sitting there, I turned and spoke to Maitreyi.

'Listen ...' I started.

'I'm not saying sorry to you,' she whispered. 'You're really mean.'

'So are you,' I whispered back.

She seemed satisfied with this. 'I wanted to say, I guess this project isn't happening anymore. I'm asking Tanveen Miss to let me do something else on my own or to put me in another group.'

'Fine,' she said, gritting her teeth. 'Ayesha's not talking to me anyway. Did Mahrukh say anything to you?'

'No.'

'Good!' she said, loudly, which woke up the sad man.

After we had both been asked, very quietly, to leave, we found ourselves standing outside with nothing to do. Maitreyi positioned herself behind a tree so that her mother wouldn't spot her and realise that she had been thrown out of dance-yoga.

'I'm so angry with Mahrukh,' she said. 'She doesn't even care that we got lost in the woods. I'm angry with you too,' she quickly pointed out, in case I got the wrong idea. 'But I'm really angry with her.'

Just then, Indu Miss walked by and Maitreyi quickly ducked behind the tree again. When she was gone, I told Maitreyi, 'You can come out now.'

'She'll come back,' she said. 'I need a better hiding place.'

'I'm going to the library,' I told her.

'Good idea! I'll come with you.'

I found this a bit strange considering she didn't want anything to do with me, but I figured we wouldn't have to talk if we were in the library. I was only going because I wanted to meet Miss Zaveri.

Miss Z was the nicest grown up I knew. She was very old and had been the librarian at the school since we were little. She had always been a kind of friend to me and Pallavi, although she didn't talk much to most people, which might have been because most people found her a little strange. She loved to talk to us, though.

We would routinely complain to her about our classes and teachers and parents. The best thing about Miss Z was that she never seemed to want to give us any advice. After we were done complaining, she would tell us about something that happened to her, or to someone she knew, which often had something to do with what we had said, but not always. If she was in a good mood that day, she would go off into all kinds of other subjects, so that by the end of the conversation we would have practically no idea where it had started.

I decided that she was exactly the kind of company I needed. She waved to us as we walked in. Maitreyi gave her a quick wave and dived behind a particularly large bookshelf.

'Your friend was in a hurry,' Miss Z observed.

'She's not my friend,' I told her, settling down in a chair nearby. 'We're just in the same group for a project together. We were,' I corrected myself.

'Don't you have work to do? I thought they were keeping all of you very busy this week.'

Miss Z always referred to the teachers as 'them', or 'those people', but not in a mean way. I once asked her why she was a librarian and not a teacher at the school. 'Oh, I can't do all the things that they do,' she had said dismissively, and had proceeded to show us, very excitedly, the new cataloguing system for the encyclopaedias. I often wondered if Miss Z had other librarian friends. I pictured them drinking tea and talking for hours about things no one else could understand, like my parents did with their friends from work.

'I got kicked out of dance-yoga,' I told her sheepishly.

'Dance-yoga?' she laughed. 'Well, I'm sure it's for the best.'

'What are those?' I asked her, pointing to a large pile of very old-looking books that I hadn't seen before.

'They belong to the old Trust,' she said. 'They've been here for ages, no one really looks at them. We were going to give them back, but the principal decided that they should stay here.'

'I don't like her,' I said, suddenly.

'Who?'

'The principal. It's her fault I had to do dance-yoga, it's her fault that I had to do a project and so it's her fault that I'm going to fail now!' I burst out.

'I don't think those people will let you fail Class VII,' pointed out Miss Z reasonably.

'They won't have a choice,' I said, tearfully, and told her the whole story, but in a low voice so that Maitreyi, who was at the other end of the very long narrow room that was the library, wouldn't hear me.

'Hmm,' she said, after listening gravely to everything I had said. 'When I was in school I wrote an essay on butterflies.'

I nodded interestedly, and we sat in silence for a minute or so as she flipped through the library record book. In the meantime, Maitreyi, who had been hiding in the reference section, had got bored. We watched as she crawled over to where the books of historical fiction were kept. I waited until she was out of earshot before I started talking again.

'Ours is on food,' I said eventually. 'Was. It was going to be good, too. Really good. We were going to talk to everybody in the city about their food habits. Everybody,' I said, embellishing freely now that I wouldn't be able to do it anymore.

'That's a lot of people,' she agreed. 'I have something you might still be interested in, though.' She pulled out one of the very old-looking books from the pile behind her. It was a big, thick leather-bound diary, and it was falling apart. She handed it to me very carefully.

'What is it?' I asked.

'Open it and see,' she told me. 'It belonged to the first principal of this school.'

We all knew the story of how our school was started. A woman called Madhavi Sultania, who was from a very rich family, decided one day that there should be a school for girls in Lailapaani. She was rich because her family used to own a jam factory, which was the biggest one here for a long time. The name of the company was Lyle & Penny, which is how the town started to be called Lailapaani. This was many, many years ago, when the only school in town was the Baldwin Boys' School. In those days, the girls from here had to go to the school in the next town. Madhavi's family didn't want her to but she did it anyway, with very little money to start with. After she died, some relatives decided to continue to run it themselves. That is, until they went broke recently.

I turned the pages of the diary and saw that it was full of handwritten recipes. The pages were yellowing and the ink had smudged in a lot of places. Some of the dishes were regular ones, but many of the recipes were for things I had never even heard of. In between, there were a few diary entries–mostly grocery lists, but also some in which she had written down what she had done during the day, and small notes and reminders. One page simply said, 'Tell RM it's not happening.'

It was the coolest thing I had ever seen.

'Why do you have a book of recipes written by her?' I asked Miss Z.

'We have all her journals and diaries,' she said. 'She used to collect recipes from different people who lived all over town and who came from different places to live here. She was really well known for her cooking. After she died, she left them with the school.'

'Can I look at it properly?' I asked Miss Z.

'Yes,' she said, turning back to her work.

The book had all sorts of stuff in it–little notes, and recipes for different kinds of things. There were even several pages filled with different recipes for jam and preserves. Some of jam recipes had been typed with a typewriter and stuck into the journal. Next to some of them, Madhavi had jotted down people's names, probably the people she had gotten the recipe from.

I was beginning to get an idea. If I could convince the others, we could still do our project on food, but make it about Madhavi Sultania. I was sure Tanveen Miss wouldn't let me do it on my own and if I joined another group, I'd have to work on another topic. There were so many stories about Madhavi Sultania that we had heard over the years that I was sure we would get really high grades for writing our project about her. If I could convince Miss Z to give me the journal for a while, I was sure the others would agree

'I guess it's not much use to you now,' said Miss Z, beginning to put all the books away.

'What if we still do the project?' I asked her. 'Will you let us borrow the book? Please?'

Miss Z looked doubtful. 'These aren't usually taken out of the library,' she said.

'No one will notice! You said yourself that no one ever looks at those books. I've never lost a library book, ever! I promise I'll take care of it, promise, promise ...' I begged.

It took a little more begging, but Miss Z finally gave in, on several conditions, including that I wouldn't let anyone else take it home.

I went over to where Maitreyi was reading.

'I have to show you something,' I told her.

She was as excited as I had been, after looking through the journal. We agreed to speak to the other two.

'You speak to Mahrukh,' she said. 'I'm not talking to her. Anyway, I don't think she'll want to, since she hates us so much.' Maitreyi was obviously not going to forgive Mahrukh in a hurry.

'I'll speak to her if you speak to Ayesha,' I agreed. I just needed them to say yes. I had no intention of being any friendlier than necessary, and I definitely didn't want to be the one to ask Ayesha for anything.

We parted ways on reasonably good terms. One down, I thought. I wasn't looking forward to meeting Mahrukh, but it had to be done.

I went to Empire Stores after school, hoping I would find her there, and I did. She was hanging around at the counter with her mother, who was dealing with the customers.

Her mother saw me come in. 'Hello, Elizabeth!' she said. 'How are your parents?'

'They're fine,' I said. Mahrukh didn't say anything.

'And is school going well?'

'Yes aunty, very well,' I lied, looking at Mahrukh significantly. She sighed deeply and walked out from behind the counter.

'We're just coming, Ma,' she said, and I followed her to the part of the store where the biscuits were kept.

'Have you come to yell again?' she asked, before I could say anything.

I counted to ten in my head. 'No,' I told her. 'I've come to ask about the project.'

'Are we still doing that thing?' she asked me. 'I thought you three would be too angry with each other to be in the same room.'

She was in for a nasty surprise when she met Maitreyi, I thought, but I didn't say so. I told her about Madhavi

Sultania's journal instead, and that Maitreyi had agreed to go ahead with the project and hopefully Ayesha would too.

'So you have the book with you?'

'That's what I'm saying!' I said. 'It's really great, and we'll be able to get our project done in no time.'

'Fine. I already asked Rajni if I could be in her group, but I'll tell them no. What are you looking for?' she asked suddenly, looking at a man who had come into the shop a while ago and had spent the last five minutes observing the shelves carefully without picking up anything. He had giggled when Mahrukh asked me if I was going to start yelling, but we had ignored him.

He looked startled. 'Um, I think some biscuits,' he said, finally.

'They're right in front of you,' Mahrukh told him.

'Right. Thanks,' he said, and scurried away.

'Must be another tourist,' said Mahrukh. 'Fine, I'll do the project. Only on one condition—no more screaming at each other without any reason. I was really irritated with you all yesterday.'

'Irritated with us?' I asked. 'You were the one that left us there. We got lost! We had to come back in the rain!'

'How could you get lost?' she asked, sounding surprised. 'I showed you how to get there!'

I decided to let Maitreyi deal with her later. 'Well, we did. But never mind that, we'll talk in school tomorrow.'

We went back to the counter, where Mahrukh's mum said, 'There you are! Go get me some paper bags from the back.'

The poor man whom Mahrukh had snapped at was paying for his things. He smiled at us, and Mahrukh scowled back at him. She didn't like tourists very much, because she said they messed up the woods.

'Sweet kids,' he said to her mother, sounding doubtful.

8

We had a three-day break for Diwali, and Ayesha was not going home.

'My parents don't want me around,' she said, when I asked.

'They've gone to the US, because her father had to travel on work and her mother wanted to visit her sister,' Maitreyi explained, rolling her eyes. 'So much drama.'

'Whatever,' Ayesha mumbled and refused to speak about it anymore.

Maitreyi, Ayesha and Mahrukh had come over to my house on the first day of the Diwali break. Ayesha, once we got past the conversation about going home, was being genuinely pleasant. Maitreyi was making a big show of being civil to Mahrukh who, if she noticed, was pretending not to. Things could have been a lot worse.

My father, who had come home early from work, was delighted to see that I had friends over. He kept fussing over them, offering them any and all of the food we had in the house. I hurried them into my room before he could embarrass me any further, but he followed us.

'Tea and fruit!' he chirped, bringing everything in on a tray and placing it on my bed.

'I'm not allowed to drink tea,' said Maitreyi, apologetically.

My father looked confused. My parents drank tea in bucketfuls every morning, and I could still remember my first cup, from when I was four. After that first time, my parents had never been able to convince me to drink milk in the mornings again.

'I don't think we have any soft drinks,' he said, sounding upset.

'Oh, that's all right,' said Maitreyi cheerfully. 'I'm not allowed to drink those either.'

'We're trying to work!' I said loudly, shutting the door in my father's face.

'I want to see the journal,' Ayesha said. 'That's why we're here, right?'

I pulled the journal out from under my bed, where I had kept it carefully, wrapped in newspaper. We pored over it with care. It looked even more magical now that it was in my house. We had to be really careful with the pages, which were crumbling in places.

'So what's the deal with this woman?' Ayesha asked.

'She started the school,' Maitreyi explained to her patiently.

'I know that,' said Ayesha. 'Why do we need to do a project on her?'

Mahrukh and I began telling them all the stories we knew about Madhavi Sultania. She was kind of a local legend. She had not only started the school, but was supposed to have helped build a lot of other places around town as well. She had even put together a book full of pictures of all the birds that came to the area. I knew this because my father once showed it to me on one of our trips to the Lailapaani Public Library when I was little.

'I heard that she once got lost in the woods while bird-watching. She built a tree house and lived there for a week!' Mahrukh said.

'Yes, it's very easy to get lost in those woods,' said Maitreyi, narrowing her eyes.

Mahrukh told us another story she had heard—how Madhavi Sultania used to love going to other people's houses for dinner, and take home their family recipes with her. Then she would make the dishes herself and invite them home to try them.

'Her family had come and settled here over a hundred years ago, when there was only a little village, and started the jam factory,' I told the others. 'Madhavi apparently told her father that she wanted to start a school for girls, because there wasn't one in the town. He said no, and they had a big fight, so she went ahead and started it herself. It was pretty small to start with, and then when her father died she took all his money and made it bigger.'

'She was the principal of the school for twenty-five years,' Mahrukh continued. 'Then something happened to her and she couldn't run the school anymore. That's when her nephew took over the school and convinced the rest of the family to continue running it. She died soon after that.'

‘When did she die?’ asked Ayesha.

‘Long back,’ I said, never having been very good with dates.

‘How?’ asked Maitreyi.

‘I don’t know for sure,’ said Mahrukh spookily. ‘But some people say she went mad. And killed herself.’

‘She didn’t,’ I told the others, who were staring at Mahrukh wide-eyed. ‘She died of cancer or something. My father told me.’

‘That’s impossible,’ scoffed Ayesha, who obviously preferred Mahrukh’s version. ‘They didn’t have cancer in olden times.’

‘They did. I know about lots of people who had cancer in those days,’ I bluffed.

‘No, they didn’t,’ said Maitreyi, jumping in. ‘It was because of their food. They used to eat lots of fruit and vegetables and healthy things. You don’t get sick if you eat fruit, my Life Instructor at my last school told me that.’

‘We eat fruit now,’ said Mahrukh, her mouth full of grapes.

This led to a long argument about whether people in the olden days ate more vegetables, then about which vegetables made you less sick, and Madhavi Sultania and her possibly tragic death were, for a while, forgotten.

The next day, all of us went to Mahrukh’s shop and we lit some sparklers and ate the muffins that they made in the bakery behind the shop. They were special Diwali muffins—each of them had a flame made of yellow cream on top, so that they looked like diyas. The cream was flavoured with mango preserves, and was delicious.

It was quite a lame celebration, I suppose, but we giggled and argued and it was a lot of fun. I thought of Pallavi in Baroda, surrounded by relatives, and for once, I didn't feel that combination of anger, fear and sadness that came over me whenever I thought about her.

Mahrukh and Maitreyi had both been really excited for days. Sports Day was always held in the middle of the first term, and while I had been half expecting Palak Nanda to cancel it for some silly philosophical reason, she had announced that it would happen after the Diwali break this year.

Our school's Sports Day had always been pretty standard. There were usually some matches—basketball, football and all that—and races. The only time I ran in one of the races, I fell down and scratched both my knees, so I never did it again. Pallavi, on the other hand, was one of the fastest runners in the school, so she always competed in the races, and often won.

The weather was always great this time of year, so even without Pallavi around, I was looking forward to Sports Day. The rules tended to be relaxed quite a bit and we could wander around the whole day, doing whatever we wanted. Plus, we didn't need to bring tiffin boxes and we got to eat lots of cake and chips instead.

Naturally, though, Sports Day wasn't going to go on 'as usual', like Palak Nanda had assured us. Two weeks before it was supposed to happen, we found ourselves in class as Tanveen Miss explained the changes that Palak Nanda had in mind. Palak Nanda had dropped in as well, to 'see how everyone was doing'.

'Dr Nanda believes, and many of us agree, that Sports Day has a tendency to leave people out,' Tanveen Miss said. 'This year, we need to come up with a plan that makes sure that everybody can play.'

No, no, no, I thought. This was absolutely the last thing I wanted. But I remembered that Tanveen Miss valued our opinions these days, so I put up my hand.

'Yes, Elizabeth?'

'What if someone doesn't want to play?' I asked tentatively.

'Ah! Well, that's exactly it,' she exclaimed. 'Maybe the reason you don't want to play is that we don't have the right kind of games. Dr Nanda has said that we should come up with new games and competitions, so that it's all about participation in goal-oriented activities as a community. Doesn't that sound just wonderful?' she asked, talking to us but smiling broadly at Palak Nanda.

'But what about sports?' asked Rajni who, for someone who was really lazy, was actually good at almost all sports.

'We'll continue to have those,' Palak Nanda assured her. 'But we feel that this could be an opportunity to broaden our horizons. For one thing, anyone who wants to play a game can play it. So far, only the best players have been allowed to play the sports that we have at this school. From now on, anyone can join any team they want,' she told us. 'Yes?' she asked Suchi, who was waving her hand in the air.

'I think that's a great idea. Otherwise, some girls are just really snobbish and don't let others play, even if they're really, really good.'

There were a few groans from the girls who played basketball. They had just managed to get Suchi thrown out of the team after the incident with the basketball hoop. She had a reputation for being competitive, and had already been given two warnings by the sports teacher last year for pushing and hitting people in the middle of the match. Palak Nanda, of course, didn't know all this, and told Suchi that snobbishness is bad and that she was very much looking forward to seeing her play this year. Mahrukh rolled her eyes at Suchi, who looked defiantly back at her.

Tanveen Miss started to make a list on the blackboard with everyone's suggestions.

'What about kho-kho?' asked Maitreyi. 'They used to play it at my old school.' Tanveen Miss wrote it on the board and Palak Nanda nodded approvingly at Maitreyi.

'Tree-climbing competition?' ventured Rakshita, pointlessly. Tanveen Miss didn't write that on the board.

'Miss, can we do a fashion show?' asked Tarini, who was sitting right in front of me.

Palak Nanda stared at her for a moment.

'Chee! I don't want to do a stupid fashion show!' shouted Ayesha from across the room.

'So who asked you to do it?' retorted Tarini.

'I want to do a rap contest,' said Ayesha.

'Okay, you can do a rap contest, I'll do a fashion show,' agreed Tarini, amiably.

'Wait!' Palak Nanda interrupted. 'Everyone, write down one activity you would like to have included. *We* will decide what will finally be played on Sports Day.' She looked at Tanveen Miss. 'Looks like you've got everything under control.' She smiled and left to speak to some other class.

I didn't want either a rap contest or a fashion show, and I didn't know how to play kho-kho. Some genius had suggested snakes and ladders. There was really no game I wanted to play. I tore off a piece of paper from my notebook and neatly wrote 'hide-and-seek' on it. I showed my chit to Rakshita, who was a little annoyed that her suggestion had been dismissed so easily. She laughed, wrote on her piece of paper and showed it to me. 'Samesame,' she said.

The next day, I was sitting and eating lunch with Mahrukh and Rakshita in the classroom.

'They've put the list up!' said Maitreyi, poking her head into the room.

'List?' asked Rakshita, finishing off her curd rice.

'The list for Sports Day,' said Maitreyi. 'They've included my suggestion!'

'So, Maitreyi was apparently a kho-kho champion at her other school,' said Ayesha, walking in.

'Ayesha's promised to join,' said Maitreyi. 'Elizabeth, why don't you? I know Mahrukh's going to be playing basketball.' Mahrukh nodded.

'Let's see,' I said, not meaning to at all.

'What else is there?' asked Mahrukh.

'A hide-and-seek tournament,' said Ayesha. 'I don't even know what that is.'

'What?' I asked, coughing because I was still swallowing my food. Rakshita looked at me delightedly.

'Who would play that?' asked Mahrukh.

Not only was hide-and-seek actually there, it had the longest list of people signing up to play it.

'Who would even suggest something like this?' wondered Maitreyi, peering at the list.

'I think I did,' I told her. She looked at me in disbelief. 'It was a joke, I didn't actually think they'd do it. And Rakshita wrote it down too; it wasn't just me, okay?'

'Hide-and-seek! Now you have to take part!' Ayesha said, poking me. 'I'll join you.'

'You can't play hide-and-seek,' objected Maitreyi. 'You said you would play kho-kho with me.'

'Let's all play kho-kho first and then join the hide-and-seek tournament,' Ayesha offered.

Mahrukh, in the meantime, was reading the board very carefully, running her finger down the list.

'What's wrong?' I asked her.

'Sheela, Tarini, Monica. I knew it, I knew it,' she muttered.

'Who?' asked Ayesha.

'Her friends from the basketball team,' I told her. 'They've signed up?' I asked Mahrukh.

'I was talking to them about Sports Day today and they said they don't know about basketball this year,' she said, fuming. 'They're not playing, they've signed up for ... for *hide-and-seek?*'

'Oh no,' said Maitreyi, patting Mahrukh on the shoulder. 'Maybe you should join the kho-kho team. You'd be really good.'

'This,' said Mahrukh, pointing at me, 'is all your fault.'

'How is it my fault?' I asked her. 'Maybe you should make basketball more fun, if you want more people to join.' I was suddenly feeling very pleased that I had chosen something so many people wanted to play.

Mahrukh walked off in a huff. Later, we saw her speaking urgently to Ahona-Mona. They were one year below us, and best friends. It was a widely known fact that Mona would do anything Ahona did. Mahrukh stomped back to us, looking even more upset.

'Palak Nanda's insisting on hide-and-seek,' she informed us. 'She says it'll build teamwork. Thanks a lot!' she said, looking at me.

When Sports Day finally came, though, Mahrukh was in a good mood again. A few new people had joined basketball, and they had spent several days practising. I was stuck in that hide-and-seek tournament and, to Maitreyi's dismay, Ayesha had joined me. When we went to play, we met Suchi, who had come along.

'What are you doing here?' asked Ayesha.

'Basketball's stupid,' she said, sulkily. Mahrukh had told us that no one wanted her on their team, but I was surprised that something like that could put Suchi off.

There was a lot of excitement about the game. There were two teams, one hiding and one seeking, and whoever lasted the first round without being found would go on to the next round. It sounded like great fun, but it wasn't.

There were so many people playing that there were vicious fights over the more obvious places to hide, and some girls who hid in the less obvious places were never found and wandered out long after the game was finished, wondering what was happening. Two girls were punished by Indu Miss for climbing trees.

Ayesha and I were on the seeking team for the first round, but when it was clear that the game was turning into a mess and a bunch of teachers were being called in to handle the situation, we decided to slip off and go for a walk. Palak Nanda had set up stalls all over the school, so we headed for those.

We had never had a Sports Day like this. There were stalls for all kinds of things—juice, food, homemade toys, everything. We spotted a stall with homemade pickles and jams, and the woman selling it looked very familiar, but I couldn't quite place her.

Ayesha and I decided to have a look at the kho-kho match. Maitreyi was spectacular—I didn't really know anything about kho-kho, but even I could tell she was really good. I was enjoying just watching and cheering her on, but Ayesha was looking nervous.

'Let's go,' she said. 'If she sees us, she'll make us play.'

We decided to go and eat vadas at one of the stalls. It was run by a friend of my parents, Sheela Aunty. She gave us a lot of extra tomato chutney, which Ayesha loved.

Eventually, Mahrukh joined us, looking sweaty. 'How was the match?' I asked her.

'Good,' she said, panting. 'We lost.'

One of the coolest things about Mahrukh was how much

she loved playing and how little she cared about whether or not her team won. She wasn't even one of the best players. On the bright side she didn't seem mad at me anymore. She proceeded to eat five vadas very quickly.

'By the way,' I asked her. 'Who's that?'

She looked towards the pickle stand, where I was pointing.

'That's Suman Sultania, stupid,' she said with her mouth full. 'How do you not know her?'

I had seen her around many times—she was Madhavi Sultania's granddaughter, and she lived in a house somewhere just outside the main town area. She had always lived here, and everyone knew her. Madhavi Sultania's granddaughter still sold jams, long after her family's factory shut down. They were not Lyle & Penny jams; she made them herself at home and they were delicious and very expensive. My parents sometimes bought some around Christmas, as a treat.

Ayesha brightened. 'We should talk to her about the project!' she said. 'Elizabeth, go talk to her.'

'No, not me,' I said, feeling shy.

'You go,' Mahrukh told her, showing no desire to abandon her plate of vadas.

'I don't even know her,' said Ayesha.

'So? It's not like she knows us,' Mahrukh pointed out, and I nodded my head furiously.

'Fine,' said Ayesha, miffed. She went over to the jam and pickle stall and we watched as she spoke to Suman Sultania for five minutes. She came back holding a jar of mango preserve.

‘See? That was easy, I just told her we wanted to do a project about her grandmother. She said come see me. And I bought this. She makes them herself, grows stuff in her garden,’ she told us proudly.

‘Let me see,’ Mahrukh said, grabbing the bottle. She sniffed at it. ‘It smells awesome.’

‘It’s not for you. It’s for me, because I talked to her.’

‘I’m sure you’ll give some to Maitreyi!’ objected Mahrukh.

‘Because she has to eat hostel food, like me,’ said Ayesha, putting the bottle away carefully.

Maitreyi’s team, of course, had won the kho-kho tournament. She had also scraped her knee badly, which meant that she and Ayesha had to go immediately back to their hostel and managed to skip Palak Nanda’s ‘concluding statement’. Palak Nanda looked really tired and sweaty, too, because she had insisted on participating in the basketball match. She began by thanking the students for allowing her to ‘share their joy’.

‘Oh, please,’ said Mahrukh, who was sitting next to me, rolling her eyes.

‘Was she terrible?’ I asked, delighted.

‘No, she’s actually good. It just made everyone feel really awkward. No one wanted to take the ball away from her.’

I tried to imagine Palak Nanda playing basketball, and wished that I had gone to watch. She had even come dressed for it, in a pair of baby-pink tracksuit pants.

Unfortunately, Palak Nanda’s plan to get everyone to join in the discussion had gone awry, since everyone was so upset at what had happened to the hide-and-seek tournament.

'That may have been somewhat ... misjudged,' she was admitting, to an irate group of Class V students, who had just finished scolding her. They had been very keen on winning the prize, until Palak Nanda reminded them that there was no prize and that playing was a reward in itself, which had made them even more angry.

'*Last* year,' said a small girl with two ponytails, obviously their leader, 'I got a trophy.'

'That's wonderful!' said Palak Nanda encouragingly, missing the point

10

With Tanveen Miss's permission, we were allowed to leave school early the next day to work on our project.

Suman Sultania's house was not very far away, but it was still outside the main town area. Maitreyi and I sat together on the bus, going over the very short list of questions we had planned to ask Madhavi's granddaughter. Mahrukh and Ayesha were in the seat in front of us.

Maitreyi had brought a little notebook in which everything was to be written down. 'Observation is very important,' she had told us. We had decided that we would take turns observing things. Maitreyi had the notebook for the first part of the day, and was diligently making a list of everything she saw during the bus ride.

Suman Sultania lived in a big, old house with a huge garden. She was sitting on a chair in the garden, reading a book. She called out when she saw us. She was old, around our grandparents' age, and very small and skinny.

'You were the girls who called about the school project,' she informed us cheerfully. We nodded, agreeing.

Maitreyi was the first one to speak. 'Miss, we wanted to ask you a few questions.'

'You can call me Suman,' she said. 'I'm not one of your teachers.'

She invited us in for tea. Maitreyi got a glass of disgusting-looking green vegetable juice, but she seemed very happy with it. Suman scurried around very quickly, and appeared with a plate of biscuits to go with the tea, which were delicious.

'Tell me more about your project,' she said.

We told her that we wanted to find out more about her grandmother's cooking. She seemed amused and puzzled by our request.

'That's very odd,' she said. 'She loved to cook, of course, but hardly anyone remembers that. Especially people your age.'

'Our librarian told us about it,' I said.

I pulled the journal out of my school bag. It was still wrapped in newspaper. Suman leaned forward, curious. When she realised what it was, she almost couldn't believe it.

'Where on earth did you get that?' she asked, very surprised.

'It was in the library at school,' explained Maitreyi. 'Our librarian gave it to us.'

'To borrow,' I added quickly. 'We'll give it back in a few days, of course. We needed to read it properly.' I handed her the journal.

'This is amazing,' she breathed, looking through the pages. 'I had no idea that she had written all this down. I've never seen this one.'

'How come you haven't seen it?' asked Ayesha accusingly. I looked at her, startled by her tone. 'Maybe it's a fake,' she whispered to me.

Suman heard her and laughed. 'I don't think anyone would try to forge a book of recipes,' she said. 'Anyway, I haven't read all the notebooks. There are so many. I've looked through a lot of them many times, but that was years ago. This one is fascinating, though. Look, she's even written down names of the people she learned them from! That should be useful to you, don't you think?'

'We could go ask them!' said Ayesha, excitedly.

'Obviously not, they're dead,' said Mahrukh, looking at her witheringly. 'Ow!' she shouted, rubbing her arm. Maitreyi had pinched her.

'They're probably dead,' agreed Suman. 'But their families are still around. Most of them are, at least.'

'Where's your family?' I asked her.

'Everyone moved out of Lailapaani,' she told me. 'They went off to other places. They still visit—a little too often for my liking, to be honest. My father moved out for a short while as well after he got married, but then we came back to live here. That was when my father's cousin was principal of the school, and he had set up a Trust so the school would run properly long after he retired, which was good because the family's money didn't last very long after that.'

'Did someone steal it?' I asked.

'No, no one stole it, but the factory finances were mismanaged. Business went badly, and people started fighting. Some of our relatives were still angry with my grandmother for spending so much money starting a school, especially because her own father hadn't wanted her to do it. Then, when her nephew finally came around and supported the idea, some of his children weren't very pleased either. Anyway, it all worked out for the best—at least the school's still running.'

I wanted to ask her more about Madhavi and the stuff with her family, but Mahrukh brought the conversation back to our project. Suman began telling us stories about the kind of food Madhavi used to make at home. She didn't have a very good memory, so she had to think a lot before she told us anything. Also, she hadn't been very close to her grandmother because, she told us, Madhavi didn't like children very much.

'But she ran a school!' said Mahrukh.

'Oh, she enjoyed that,' said Suman. 'I got the feeling she didn't think the two were related. I suppose that's fair.'

We went back to the people Madhavi had named in the book of recipes, and Suman helped us out by telling us where some of them had lived, and whether there might be people in their families who still remembered her. We chatted for a while. We found out that she had lived on her own here for about ten years, and that she used to have a job, but had taken early retirement. Now she spent a lot of time gardening, reading, hiking and making jams and pickles, of course.

'Why don't you have kids?' Ayesha demanded.

'Never wanted them. Don't like them much. I must have taken after my grandmother!' She grinned broadly as Ayesha looked offended.

She was very interested in all of us and asked us a lot of questions. I found out new things about the others. Mahrukh's older sister, who had gone off to college, had been at Hill School too and Maitreyi had never met her father because her parents had separated when she was a baby.

'I'm sorry I couldn't give you any more stories,' Suman told us apologetically. 'I'll have to think a little longer, now that I know the sort of thing you're looking for.'

Maitreyi was looking out of the window. 'Do you grow vegetables?' she asked Suman.

'Oh, yes!' she answered excitedly. 'I'll show you. In fact, why don't we take a walk? I have relatives visiting, but they've gone out for the afternoon, thank god. I'll take you up the hill nearby, it's a lovely evening. Leave your things here,' she told us. 'It's a bit of a climb.'

We wandered into the garden and examined the vegetable patch as Suman locked up locked up. Maitreyi was just scribbling away in her notebook. I wondered what she was writing, so I tried to take a peek.

'Stop reading over my shoulder,' said Maitreyi.

'Why do you have to list all the vegetables she's growing? Just write the important stuff,' I told her.

'The project's about food, isn't it? Anyway, it's my turn. When it's your turn, you write what you think is important.'

'Let's go!' yelled Suman, emerging from the house.

The walk was definitely more than 'a bit of a climb'. It

was an hour long. Ayesha and I were the slowest. Suman Sultania could climb quicker than any old person I had ever seen. Mahrukh was even quicker, but she kept pausing to wait for the rest of us to catch up. Suman was not that considerate, however.

'Come on, you two!' she shouted happily. 'I can understand that Ayesha's not used to it, but you have no excuse, Elizabeth! Ayesha, isn't this place lovely?'

'No,' said Ayesha firmly, panting.

By the time we got back down the hill, we were all tired and famished. We were fed a snack of biscuits and paranthas and sent off.

Maitreyi and I fell asleep on the bus ride home, and Mahrukh had to wake me up when our stop came. I walked Mahrukh home and then went on to my place, remembering that my parents had gone out to meet some friends. I pulled the key out from under a flower pot and let myself into the house.

I decided to get started on the essay that Indu Miss had asked me to write. I had hoped that she would forget, but at the end of our last class she had said, 'I'm still waiting for that essay, Elizabeth!' wagging her finger at me threateningly.

First, though, I would have to keep the book of recipes under my bed, where it would be safe. I opened my school bag, which was heavy and full of rubbish as usual—various books that I was reading, school books, bits of paper and empty packets of chips. I searched through my bag, pulling out things one by one, at first calmly and then more frantically, until I could no longer deny that the book was not there.

11

'What's gone?' my mother asked, for the sixth time.

I started wailing even more loudly. My mother put her head in her hands and my father soundlessly handed me a glass of water, which I didn't take. They were running out of things to do.

When I realised the journal wasn't in my bag anymore, my hands had gone completely cold. I looked around my room numbly, knowing, of course, that there was no way I would find it in the house. It had been in my bag all day, but I looked under my bed a dozen times and in all the cupboards and shelves I could find, simply to try and delay the inevitable realisation that I had, in fact, lost it.

Desperately, I considered my options. Maybe I could fake it, I thought. Even Suman Sultania hadn't read the book, so there was certainly a chance that no one had looked at it in years. If I could copy her handwriting ... The stupidity of this idea had hit me as soon as I had thought it. I was terrible at copying other people's handwriting and even worse at lying. There was nothing to do but to admit that I had lost it.

What would happen to me then? I would probably get expelled. Maybe they would think I had stolen it. Hopefully, I wouldn't go to jail—I didn't know what the penalty was for stealing precious historical documents. I was too young, so they wouldn't send me to jail. Maybe they would send one of my parents instead. Which one? Maybe they would make me choose, as punishment. The awfulness of that thought had sent my head spiralling, and I had started weeping uncontrollably.

I had been unable to stop even after my parents came home. They waited patiently until I was done.

Eventually, the tears stopped.

'What happened?' my mother asked finally.

'I did something bad,' I said, managing to choke out some dry sobs.

'What did you do?'

I thought quickly. I couldn't bring myself to tell them what had happened, although I knew they would have to find out sooner or later. I gave a loud sniff, long and disgusting because my nose was running.

'I lost a book. A ... l-library book,' I told them.

'Is that all?' my mother said, relieved. 'The way you were crying, I thought you'd killed someone, or worse.'

'Go to sleep, you'll feel better,' said my father, whose answer to all of life's problems was a quick nap.

I didn't have the heart to tell him this problem wouldn't be gone in the morning. Still, I went to bed. Outside, I could hear worried whispering as my parents wondered what was wrong with me.

Predictably, it was a bad night. I lay awake for hours, terrified, running all sorts of scenarios in my head, which got weirder and weirder as I drifted off to sleep. I had dreams of disappointed grown ups and angry twelve-year-olds and, at one point, Madhavi Sultania herself made an appearance, sitting in a tree house and screaming down at me.

'Where has it gone?' demanded Ayesha, the next day at school. We were sitting on a bench behind the basketball court. I had called an emergency meeting.

'I don't know where it's gone, that's the point,' I told her in frustration.

'Did you check everywhere?' asked Maitreyi, uselessly. 'You had it with you the entire time!'

'I remember putting it in my bag after showing it to Suman. It was before we went for a walk. Then I picked the bag up and left with all of you.'

'Did it feel lighter?' asked Mahrukh.

'How should I remember?' I burst out. 'It's gone, that's all! There's nowhere it could possibly be that I haven't checked already!'

'Okay,' said Maitreyi. 'Could you have lost it in the bus?'

'It's possible,' I admitted. 'We were asleep. But that means someone stole it.'

'Why would someone steal a book like that?' asked Mahrukh sensibly. We thought about it for a while.

'It's obvious now,' said Ayesha quietly. We all turned towards her.

'Are you saying ...' began Maitreyi.

'Yes,' said Ayesha, looking at her. 'Suman Sultania stole the book.'

I protested. 'No way! Why would she? She was so nice to us!'

'It makes perfect sense,' Maitreyi explained to me patiently. 'She had never seen the book before, and she was really surprised that we had it. She was the only one, apart from the four of us, who knew that it was in your bag. When we went outside to the garden, she could easily have taken it.'

I refused to believe her. 'That makes no sense. Why would she steal it? It's her grandmother's journal. If she wanted it, she could have just taken it back from the school.'

'Maybe she's gone crazy,' suggested Ayesha. 'The way Madhavi did. Did you see the way she was running up and down that hill?'

'Maybe,' Mahrukh conceded. 'Or maybe she can't have it back. Didn't Miss Z tell you that Palak Nanda wanted the books to stay in the library? Maybe Suman wants them but can't get them, and when she found this one with us, she couldn't resist. Anyway, the fact is that Maitreyi is right. No one else could have known where it was, and you're saying you definitely put it in your bag. Are you sure?'

'Yes!' I cried. 'I'm sure. And this is all pointless, because *I have lost it*. I'm just going to go tell Miss Z now, and let them do what they want to me, I don't care.' I had tears running down my cheeks by then, and I didn't care about that either. Normally I would have been mortified at the thought of crying in front of the others.

The other three stared at me blankly.

'Don't be stupid,' said Maitreyi, finally. 'We'll get it back somehow. *Even* if she doesn't have it,' she said quickly, as I opened my mouth to protest again, 'we need to find out for sure. But she does have it. She's got to have taken it. There's no other way.'

'*No,*' I said firmly. 'I'm saying no. Let's just tell the teachers.'

'This is not just your problem, okay, Elizabeth?' said Ayesha, getting angry now. 'We're all going to get into trouble, so we all have a say in this.'

'I told Miss Z I would be responsible for the book and that I wouldn't give it to anyone else. You're not going to be in trouble, I am,' I told her.

'Look, we're not going to get into trouble, all right?' said Maitreyi. 'Not if we manage to get it back.'

'Well, if she's taken it ...' I started. The others looked triumphant. 'I'm not saying that's what happened, but *if* she has, there's nothing we can do.'

'Of course there is,' said Mahrukh impatiently.

'What?' I asked.

'We're going to break into her house and find it, of course,' said Maitreyi.

12

It was a very complicated plan. Ayesha and Mahrukh were to go and pay Suman Sultania another visit, to try and figure out ways we could get into the house. I volunteered to do this—only because I wanted to make sure they didn't do anything stupid, but they saw right through me. I was voted out of the first part of the plan because the others thought I would mess it up. The second part of the plan was to find the journal and steal it back.

Everyone (except me) was very excited, but the day before this was supposed to happen, Ayesha didn't turn up in class. Maitreyi did, but she was sniffling and wasn't looking well at all.

'Ayesha has the flu,' she told us, looking green. 'And so do I. I think we should postpone Operation Sultania until she's better,' she said, retching loudly.

Mahrukh looked repulsed. 'Maybe you should have stayed back at the hostel.'

'I wanted to, but my mother wouldn't let me. I think I'm getting worse, though.'

'Why are we calling it Operation Sultania?' I asked unsympathetically. I was secretly relieved, hoping that I would be able to convince Mahrukh against the plan while the other two were out of action. 'It's not like it could fool anybody. We're using her name.'

'I don't know. It was Ayesha's idea,' wheezed Maitreyi.

'Of course it was,' I said, rolling my eyes.

As predicted, Maitreyi had to stay in her hostel room for the next week, along with Ayesha. I begged Mahrukh to change her mind, but she didn't budge. She said that it was just as well that we would have to postpone it, because it would look too suspicious if we went and met her immediately after the journal was lost.

Unfortunately, Maitreyi and Ayesha got better by the weekend, and Operation Sultania was back on. Maitreyi was still a bit ill, so Mahrukh and I went and visited them in the hostel to discuss the plan on Saturday. I had never been inside the school hostel before. It was very bleak and depressing, with long narrow corridors.

Ayesha met us outside and took us to the room she shared with Maitreyi. We ran into Indu Miss on the way. She was wearing a kaftan with flowers on it, which somehow made her even more terrifying.

'Visitors, Ayesha?' she asked. 'Are you feeling well enough?'

'Yes, miss. We've missed classes, so we wanted to take notes and catch up,' said Ayesha piously.

'I'm glad you're taking initiative,' said Indu Miss, never missing a chance to deliver a stern moral message. 'Essay, Elizabeth!'

We scurried away into their room. Maitreyi was lying in bed, blowing her nose. Her side of the room was neat and pretty, decorated with posters from the *Harry Potter* and *Lord of the Rings* movies. Ayesha's side had posters of various pop stars whom I didn't recognise and it was messy. Even though it had been months since school had started, it almost looked like Ayesha hadn't even fully unpacked her things. There were a few clothes still spilling out of suitcases and an open trunk. I guess that she was still hoping to go back home.

'Good! You're here,' said Maitreyi cheerfully.

'How're you feeling?' I asked her, selfishly hoping she was still sick.

'Much better,' she replied. 'Mother, who at first said I should keep going to school, now thinks I should just stay in bed. She was just here.'

'I know, we saw her outside,' said Ayesha.

'We have to be careful,' said Maitreyi. 'She's been in and out of the room all day.'

'Okay, so here's the plan,' whispered Mahrukh. 'Ayesha and I will go tomorrow. I'll try and lure Suman out to the garden, so Ayesha can have a look around and see if there's another way in.'

'I had another thought,' said Ayesha. 'I think Maitreyi and Elizabeth should come with us.'

'Yes!' I said, relieved.

'Not inside, though,' said Ayesha. 'You two stay outside, and see if you can find a way in from the back. We didn't really get a chance to look that day, but I think she has a big backyard. There has to be a way in from there, and we may not be able to find an excuse to check everywhere if we're with her.'

I shook my head furiously, but Maitreyi's eyes had already lit up. 'That's a *brilliant* idea!' she exclaimed. I looked at her, appalled.

Once again, I was overruled. We were to set out the next day. Mahrukh had already called Suman and asked to meet her. She reported that Suman had sounded pleased, and had said that we were welcome to drop in anytime we felt like.

'The nerve,' muttered Ayesha, shaking her head in disbelief. 'How can she look us in the eye, after what she's done?'

'Some people just don't have feelings,' Mahrukh agreed.

The next day was a Sunday, and Mahrukh and Ayesha were to out for their meeting with Suman in the afternoon. We had decided not to all go together, in case Maitreyi and I were spotted. The two of us had headed into that part of town early, and would sneak into her backyard just after Mahrukh and Ayesha arrived. It had to be perfectly timed. We had all set our watches so that they showed the same time. Ayesha and Mahrukh would reach Suman's house at 4.30 pm, and Maitreyi and I would get there by 4.40.

There was a low fence around the back garden, and we were able to scale it easily. The back of the house was unkempt, with lots of big unruly bushes and large piles of cement and construction material. Maitreyi and I crept behind one such pile, Maitreyi trying very hard not to sneeze.

'You'll give us away!' I whispered. 'Stop sniffling.'

'I can't help it,' she whispered back, apologetically. 'Anyway, there's no one here. They're all in the house. Let's get closer to a window so we can hear what's happening. There's a wall over there, next to the window. Nobody will be able to see us.'

We got on all fours and crawled towards the wall. She was right. It was slightly broken and was jutting out next to one of the back windows. We stood directly behind it and listened hard. We could hear Ayesha's voice inside.

'That's *so* interesting,' she was saying. 'And tea sounds wonderful. Let me come into the kitchen and help you make it!' she shouted, unnecessarily loudly.

We waited. I couldn't hear anything else for a while, so I could only assume that, if Mahrukh was quietly looking around, she was doing a good job.

Soon after they were back with the tea, Ayesha convinced Suman to take her outside to the front garden to look at the plants. Mahrukh went with them and returned quickly, claiming that she had to go to the bathroom. As soon as we heard Mahrukh coming in alone, Maitreyi rapped on the window. Mahrukh, looking around to make sure she wasn't being watched, opened it for us quietly.

'Any luck?' she asked us.

'Not really,' I said. 'There doesn't seem to be any way in from here, and she's sure to see us. Can we leave now? This is pointless.'

'No!' she whispered, urgently. 'There's a huge library upstairs. That's where the book must be. She said she's going out soon, so we'll be able to search around a little more. There's a back door and I've checked that it's not locked, so you guys can get in through there.'

'While she's out?' I asked, horrified.

'What, you'd rather do it while she's here?' Maitreyi asked. 'Okay, keep her outside for a little longer. We'll come in, and head upstairs at once. You two leave with her when she goes out, and come back quickly. We'll let you in.'

'What if someone hears?' asked Mahrukh doubtfully.

'No one's going to hear!' whispered Maitreyi. 'Now make her leave soon, so that we can search.'

Mahrukh nodded and left, shutting the window behind her. We found the back door, which was on the side of the house. Once we were in, we looked around for the staircase and hurried upstairs as fast as we could without making too much noise.

Mahrukh was right—Suman had a massive library. It didn't look like it belonged in the house. The house was big, but not very fancy or anything. The library, on the other hand, was beautiful. It was full of really old books. Maitreyi and I went and hid behind one of the shelves. We didn't want to take the risk of anyone downstairs hearing us, so we decided to start looking for the stolen journal only after we were sure Suman had left.

We waited for exactly forty-three minutes, during which we heard them come back in, talk for a long time and then finally leave. I nudged Maitreyi, who was immersed in a book.

'They're gone,' I whispered. 'We should go make sure that the back door is open.'

We tiptoed down the stairs, ready to dart back up in case Suman decided to come back. There were too many ways this could go wrong, I thought. She was sure to come in, having forgotten her bag or something. I told Maitreyi this.

'Stop imagining the worst,' she snapped me.

We undid the latch on the back door and peered outside. Mahrukh and Ayesha were climbing over the fence and running towards us, trying to dodge the bushes and piles of stuff strewn all over the backyard.

We went upstairs together. There were lots of books in the library, so we divided up the place into four, so that each of us could look in one specific section.

'How long did she say she was going to be gone?' I asked.

'For a few hours,' said Mahrukh. 'She said she was meeting somebody for dinner. That gives us enough time to search the house, find the book and get out before the last bus leaves.'

We split up, searching for the book on all the shelves. Looking at all the books Suman had, I felt a little sad that she was now our enemy. If she had been a nice person, I would have loved to come and read here. There were books about all sorts of things, many of them so old that they might have belonged to Madhavi herself. There were lots about birds and animals, with big beautiful pictures and crumbling spines. I looked and looked, but I couldn't find the book of recipes.

'Anything?' I whispered across the room to Mahrukh, who was on her knees searching the lower shelves.

'Nope,' she whispered back. 'Nothing from the others, either.'

I looked around. Ayesha had given up the search and was sitting on one of the windowsills, humming something under her breath, her legs swinging around. I yanked her off.

'*Don't do that!*' I almost yelled. 'Someone outside might see!'

'There's no one,' she said calmly. 'I haven't found anything. I don't think it's here. She must have hidden it somewhere else in the house. We need to search her room or something.'

'We can't do that!' I objected.

'Look, we're already here, so we might as well. The house is empty,' said Maitreyi.

Just then, we heard a loud noise outside the library, like the sound of a door closing. We froze.

'Do you think she's home?' asked Mahrukh nervously.

'She can't be! It's too early,' said Ayesha. 'One of us needs to go and check.'

We all stared at each other, each of us hoping someone else would volunteer.

'I don't think it was the downstairs door,' said Maitreyi finally. 'It was too loud. We wouldn't be able to hear it that loudly from here.'

'Maybe it's a thief,' said Ayesha, shivering.

'You three are useless,' I said. 'This was all your idea. If you're too scared to look, I will.'

I walked quietly towards the library door, trying not to make any noise. It was an old house, so I assumed that the floorboards would be creaky. I opened the door just a little, careful to stand to one side.

There was someone else in the house.

It wasn't Suman Sultania.

I could see the back of his head as he walked down the stairs noisily. I tried not to breathe as I watched him go into into the living room and, from what I could hear, turn on the TV.

I shut the door as silently as I could and padded back to where the others were. Ayesha was clinging to Maitreyi in fear, and Mahrukh was sitting on the floor, hugging her knees. I told them what I had seen.

'It's a thief!' said Ayesha.

'He's watching TV,' I pointed out. 'A thief wouldn't do that.'

'Suman told us the last time that her relatives keep visiting,' said Maitreyi. 'Did she say if anyone was staying here today?'

Mahrukh shook her head.

'Whoever it is,' I said, 'he's sitting in the living room. There's no way we'll be able to get out now.'

Just then, we heard the front door slam. I went and peeked again, and the man seemed to have left. When I told the others, Maitreyi gave a quick 'Yippee' and crept down the stairs. Mahrukh went after her.

When they came back upstairs, their faces had gone pale.

'What happened?' asked Ayesha, trembling again.

'The back door is locked,' said Mahrukh. 'And so is the front one.'

13

'He locked it?' I asked dumbly, hardly daring to believe our terrible luck.

'He must have. It was only latched before,' said Mahrukh.

'There's no other way out?' I asked.

'No, all the windows have bars on them.'

'Oh, god. Ohgodohgodohgod,' said Ayesha, clearly freaking out now.

I had gone completely cold. I sat down and tried to calm myself. Ayesha was in the middle of a panic attack, and Maitreyi was trying to comfort her. Mahrukh was just staring at the three of us.

'It's okay,' I heard Maitreyi say. 'We'll just have to wait until someone comes back.'

'You don't get it!' wailed Ayesha. 'If they expel us, it'll be my second time. Can you imagine where my parents are going to send me next? Somewhere worse than this!'

Suddenly, a thought struck me. 'There has to be a landline!' I said. 'We can call our parents!'

'No!' said Maitreyi. 'We have to be able to get out of here on our own, somehow.'

'It doesn't matter,' said Mahrukh. 'I already checked. There is a landline phone downstairs, but it seems to be dead. There is one room, which is locked, but none of the other rooms have another phone that I could see. We're stuck, properly.'

There was a minute of miserable silence as we let this sink in. We settled down on the floor, getting ready to just wait it out.

Finally, Mahrukh spoke. 'Does anyone want tea?' she joked.

'I don't drink tea,' muttered Maitreyi automatically. Ayesha looked at her and began to laugh.

'Should I go check the kitchen?' I said, suddenly feeling reckless. The others looked at me in alarm.

A few minutes later, we were stuffing ourselves with biscuits, jalebis and some bananas I had found in Suman's fridge.

'This is awesome,' said Ayesha, looking at me approvingly. She seemed to have cheered up a little.

I shrugged. 'We're going to be in trouble anyway,' I said.

'Stop saying that, we're not going to get in any trouble,' said Maitreyi, reassuringly. 'She'll come home in time, and we'll find a way to sneak out, okay?'

I had resigned myself to the fact that that was not going to happen. Maitreyi was being optimistic. We went back upstairs and settled down to wait in the library. I couldn't stop thinking about what Ayesha had said about being expelled.

'Why did you get expelled?' I asked her.

'She won't say,' said Maitreyi.

'Why not?' I asked.

'Because it's nobody's business,' Ayesha shot back.

'Was it better or worse than this?' asked Mahrukh, clearly enjoying herself.

'It doesn't matter,' said Ayesha.

'That means it's worse!' said Mahrukh, delighted.

I tried to imagine what could be worse than breaking into someone's house and eating all their food. I'd never done anything this bad in my life.

'Fine, it's worse,' said Ayesha. Mahrukh applauded. 'But I'm not telling you anything more!'

Mahrukh needled her to go on, but she refused. Mahrukh gave up at last, saying, 'I don't think Palak Nanda would expel anyone, do you?'

'Why wouldn't she? And anyway, I'm sure Indu Miss would convince her to,' I said, giving Maitreyi the evil eye. She didn't disagree.

Ayesha looked hopeful. 'She wouldn't kick her own daughter out, I'm sure. And that means she can't throw us out either.'

'She's done worse,' said Maitreyi grimly. 'And she doesn't even know I'm out.'

'What do you mean?'

'I *mean* that she told me to stay in bed because I'm still sick. She's gone out for the day, so I sneaked out. That's why we need to get out of here ourselves, as soon as we can, before she notices that I'm gone.'

'Great,' I said, throwing my hands up in the air. 'So now she's going to be even more angry. We're finished.'

'We're not!' said Maitreyi, sounding upset.

'It's okay,' said Ayesha, sighing resignedly. 'I can deal with being thrown out again. Maybe they'll let me go back to Delhi. Anyway, it must be worse for you two; you've probably never been in trouble in your lives.'

'That's not true!' I objected, not pleased with what Ayesha obviously thought about me. 'I've been in trouble loads of times.'

'Name one,' she challenged. 'Not counting doing badly in class, or whatever.'

I thought about it, and realised that I couldn't really come up with anything. I had always been a good student, in the sense that I had never gotten into any serious trouble. Of course, my track record was about to undergo a dramatic change.

'I knew it,' Ayesha sniggered, in a way that I did not like.

'I've been in trouble,' said Maitreyi.

'Not real trouble!' said Ayesha.

The two of them began squabbling, and I joined Mahrukh, who had gotten bored of our conversation and was looking through a big book full of pictures of people in dance costumes.

I looked out of the window and saw that it was now completely dark outside. I tried to bury the panic I felt rising in my stomach, telling myself again that there was nothing more that we could possibly do. I pulled out a book from one of the library shelves and began reading. Ayesha and Maitreyi had given up on their argument.

'This is a really cool library,' Maitreyi was saying, examining one of the shelves.

'Whatever,' said Ayesha, yawning. 'I don't like books.'

'What *do* you like?' asked Mahrukh, smirking slightly.

'I like music.'

'Yeah, I saw all those pop star posters in your room,' I said.

'They're not pop stars,' Ayesha said scornfully. 'They're hip-hop artists. And I like computer stuff, though it's been months since I've even *seen* a computer. They don't believe in computers at the hostel. Not even for the internet. I had to *write* a letter to my friends in Delhi the other day. A letter!'

Maitreyi looked at her, amused. 'Why didn't you just call them on the phone?'

'Because my parents said I wasn't allowed.' She yawned again, and leaned against the wall, shutting her eyes. 'Wake me up when something happens.'

Maitreyi, Mahrukh and I were sprawled on the floor, reading. Mahrukh was trying to pick up biscuit crumbs from the floor with her fingers. I was reading an incredibly boring story, and I must have fallen asleep myself, because I was suddenly woken up when Mahrukh hit me on the head.

'OW!' I yelped, jumping to my feet.

'Hide!' whispered Mahrukh urgently, pulling me to safety

behind a chair. I could hear footsteps and loud voices in the garden.

'What happened?'

'She's back! And she's brought people with her. We're dead,' Mahrukh told me.

'What do you think she'll do to us?'

'Who knows? All we know about her is that she's a book thief. Who knows what else she is?'

I looked at my watch. It was 10 pm. My parents would be insanely worried.

'How could you let me sleep that long?' I whispered to Mahrukh furiously.

'Well, what we were we supposed to do? Nobody was home yet. We didn't know what to do either. Maitreyi's mother is going to kill her, and it's not like my parents are going to be thrilled.'

As if on cue, we heard Mahrukh's mother's voice. She was calling out our names in the garden.

I felt a strange mixture of relief and terror. On the one hand, we weren't going to die in some woman's library. On the other hand, everyone would know that we broke into her house and god knows what would happen then.

And then I heard my father's voice.

'Elizabeth! Mahrukh!' he was yelling.

There were footsteps on the staircase, and the library door opened. I recognised my father's shoes from my spot under the chair.

I got up slowly, and Mahrukh followed. He stared at us.

'What are you doing?' he asked, too surprised to say anything else.

'Hiding,' said Mahrukh, trying ridiculously to act casual.

'Are you mad?' he asked her.

By then, Maitreyi and Ayesha had emerged from where they were hiding. My father looked at them and said nothing. He turned around and walked down the stairs, and we followed him sheepishly out of the house and into the garden where Mahrukh's parents and Suman Sultania were staring at us in horror.

'But ... what ... how did you ...' stammered Suman.

Mahrukh's mother gave her a big hug, talking non-stop. 'What is wrong with you? We were so worried! What are you doing here? You came here hours ago!'

'And there were only two of them,' said Suman, peering at us doubtfully.

I observed my feet as my father began apologising to her profusely. Mahrukh and Ayesha, obviously not yet convinced of her innocence, glared at her in the dark. I heard Maitreyi sniffling.

Suman was still gaping at us with her mouth open, not knowing what to say. Finally, all she managed to get out was, 'It's okay. Just take them home ... *Please.*'

We headed home together. Maitreyi and Ayesha were dropped off at the hostel, after the school was called to make sure everyone knew they were all right. Indu Miss was standing at the gate, looking madder than I'd ever seen her.

'Get in, you two! And all of you,' she continued, turning to me and Mahrukh, 'principal's office, first thing in the morning!'

My mother, needless to say, was furious. It turned out that they had been searching for us for over an hour. Mahrukh's parents had called mine, because Mahrukh had said she was going to Suman's house for the project and they had assumed she would be going with me. They had considered the possibility that we had decided to stay for dinner, until Suman's car was spotted in town, outside a small restaurant where she was eating with her friends. She told them that Mahrukh and Ayesha had left her house hours ago.

They searched in all the places we were likely to have been in town, and finally had decided to go over to her house and check if we were still in that area Maybe, they reasoned, we had missed the bus and had had the good sense to wait in her garden or something. It hadn't crossed anyone's mind that we could have been locked into Suman's house after having entered it illegally. In desperation, my father had walked around the house calling our names, not expecting to find us there at all.

My parents managed to get the entire story out of me with no effort whatsoever—I told them everything, from Miss Z, to losing the journal, to our disastrous plan to get the book back. They stared at me, amazed.

'Why would you ever do something that stupid?' my mother spluttered.

'I don't know,' I said miserably. 'Are you going to punish me?'

My parents looked at each other. I had never done something like this before, so they didn't have any routine punishments.

'I'm getting thrown out of school tomorrow anyway, so I guess you can decide then,' I said sadly, hoping this would make them feel sorry for me. It almost looked like it was going to work, but all that my mother would say was, 'Go to bed, you're going to have a long day tomorrow.' This was not reassuring in the least.

'I feel sick,' I told my parents the next morning. It was not a lie. The thought of what awaited me at school had made my skin clammy and I thought I was going to throw up.

'Nice try,' said my mother, shoving my lunch box forcefully into my school bag.

'I wasn't trying anything,' I told her resentfully, zipping up my school bag and opening the front door. 'If you don't care that I'm sick, that's fine.'

'Not the best time to angle for sympathy,' said my father heartlessly from behind the newspaper.

I slammed the door behind me. Mahrukh was waiting for me outside her store.

Indu Miss was already with Palak Nanda when we got to the principal's office. They were in the middle of a heated discussion when we walked in.

'Miss, you called us?' said Mahrukh, the bravest among us at that moment.

'Yes, yes,' said Palak Nanda, sitting down hurriedly.

'I'll leave you to it,' said Indu Miss, leaving the room.

'Oh Indu, won't you stay?' pleaded Palak Nanda.

'I have to take a class,' she said, shutting the door behind her.

Left alone with us now, Palak Nanda looked as nervous as we did.

'I just want to begin by saying that this is upsetting, it's *very very* upsetting,' she said, really looking like she meant it.

We each looked at a spot of floor.

'I hope you don't need me to tell you how wrong it was for you to have done ... what you did?'

'No miss,' we all said.

'So now let me tell you how I feel about all this,' she began. 'I feel angry, and betrayed, and ... very *very angry*.'

I hoped like mad that she wouldn't cry, because I was as close to bawling as I could possibly get.

'You *lost a precious book*. Then you accused a lovely lady of *stealing that book*. Then you went into her house *without permission*. Then you ate all her food!' she finished.

'Sorry, miss. We were hungry, miss,' said Ayesha. I fleetingly wondered how she knew everything.

Palak Nanda looked at Ayesha, eyes narrowed. 'Do not treat me,' she said, 'like I am some kind of fool. One does not,' she continued, 'simply *get hungry*.'

I realised that she had gotten so angry that she had lost track of which part she was really angry about. It was too soon to tell if this was a good thing.

She shook her head and came back to the point. 'You betrayed our *trust*,' she said. 'You betrayed the trust of your teachers when they let you go out and do this project.'

Maitreyi rolled her eyes, but thankfully Palak Nanda did not notice.

'You betrayed the trust of a woman who graciously

allowed you into her house. You betrayed the trust of the librarian who gave you something important to keep ...'

That did it for me. I burst into tears.

'The book was my fault,' I sobbed. 'I'm really, really sorry. I was supposed to keep it carefully. It was all my fault. I should have checked. I'm so sorry. This whole thing is my fault.'

Palak Nanda was staring at me, poker-faced, clearly trying not to cry herself. She covered her face with her hands.

'The journal,' she breathed. 'Oh god, what am I going to do? The Trust will have our heads for this. Oh god. Oh god.'

I started crying again, and Palak Nanda was leaning back in her chair with her face covered, muttering curse words under her breath. The other three looked from me to her, confused.

We waited untill Palak Nanda had recovered. 'It's okay,' she told us bravely. 'I will deal with it. We will apologise to them. It's only one book,' she said, reassuring herself. 'But the four of you are not off the hook. Suman Sultania is very, very upset. She knows that you suspected her of stealing *her own grandmother's book*.'

'How did she know?' I asked.

'We told her. Indu told me,' she said, surprised. 'Of course she knows.'

We all glared at Maitreyi, who crossed her arms and looked at us defiantly.

'No, you are *not* off the hook,' continued Palak Nanda. 'It would appear that I am required to give you a punishment. I do not believe in punishment. I believe in nurturing and facilitating your path to *right action*. So this is not punishment. It is a facilitation. You will make amends to Suman Sultania, whom you have hurt terribly with your behaviour. I have invited her here to make you ... to *give you the opportunity* to show her that you are sorry.'

She motioned to us to come with her, and we stepped outside the office to the waiting room, where Suman Sultania was sitting. We stood in a line in front of her, because we didn't know how else to stand. Suman Sultania looked like she desperately wanted to leave.

I began. 'We're really sorry, miss,' I told her. 'About everything.'

'Uh, that's okay,' she said, looking longingly at the door.

'Suman has a *lovely* garden, as I am sure you have seen,' said Palak Nanda. 'And I am sure she could use a lot of help with taking care of it.'

'I suppose,' said Suman, not sure where this was going.

'You will dedicate three days a week for three weeks to helping her take care of that garden!' Palak Nanda announced, pleased with her masterpiece.

'Palak, it's really all right, I don't even spend that much time ...'

'Nonsense! Of course they will come!' said Palak Nanda, slapping Maitreyi on the back. 'I will see the four of you later,' she told us. 'And Suman, do not spare them!' She went back into her office, leaving behind an uncomfortable silence.

'You can come by tomorrow,' said Suman finally, and walked out.

14

Ayesha was gleeful as we walked towards Suman Sultania's house from the bus stop. She was particularly pleased with me.

'Obviously, it's because of you! When you started crying like that, Palak Nanda went totally soft on us. She was so mad before,' she said, when I asked her politely to stop hugging me.

Maitreyi gave me a sympathetic look. She wasn't as thrilled as Ayesha about how things worked out, because she got yelled at by Indu Miss even worse than the rest of us.

I was not feeling happy at all. After our 'meeting' with Palak Nanda, I had gone to see Miss Z to try and apologise. I was feeling so terrible about the journal that I was ready to get screamed at by her, even if it would have broken my heart.

It turned out to be even worse than I had expected, because she had been very quiet, and said only that it was her own fault and she shouldn't have given something that important to a student. It was a lot worse than getting yelled at by either Palak Nanda or Indu Miss.

'Told you she wouldn't expel us,' said Mahrukh happily, placing a colourful insect on Ayesha's shoulder. Ayesha screamed.

'Well, we've still been punished,' Maitreyi pointed out. 'We're not allowed to go anywhere apart from these gardening trips for a month.'

'Please, who cares?' said Ayesha. 'It's not like they've been letting us go where we want the rest of the time, except for project work.'

'The project!' I said, remembering.

'Oh, Tanveen Miss spoke to us about that when you weren't there,' said Mahrukh.

I had had to leave school early the previous day, after speaking to Miss Z, because I really did fall sick. I started throwing up, and I got a very real fever, which disappeared magically once I got home.

'She said we aren't allowed to go out and do it, so we have to do the entire thing reading stuff in the library. "Figure it out," she said.' Great, I thought. I'll have to spend the rest of the term sitting in the same room as Miss Z, who hates me.

When we reached Suman's house, she wasn't there. We stood nervously around the garden, waiting. Finally, she turned up at the gate.

'Ah! Why is it that every time I go out these days I find a group of children when I come back? No, no, make yourselves at home! You know where the kitchen is,' she said, hurrying into the garden and cackling.

We spent most of our time hanging around on the grass and going on hikes. Suman didn't need that much work done, so after we were done watering the plants, occasionally planting a few things and cleaning up some of the messy backyard, we went on walks with Suman, who was quite happy to order us around the garden and yell at us to walk faster on hikes.

'Be careful with that!' yelled Suman to me, as I struggled with a large potted plant that needed shifting. She was sitting in the sun reading a magazine. Mahrukh threw an earthworm at Maitreyi, who responded by sitting on her and putting mud in her hair. Suman looked away and yawned.

Suddenly, a young man came out of the house. He looked slightly dishevelled and he was wearing shorts.

'Who's that?' whispered Ayesha.

'I don't know,' I said, then suddenly remembered the feet I saw coming down the stairs while we were hiding in the library. I looked carefully at his feet, and recognised them. 'It's the guy who was in the house the other day,' I told Ayesha Ayesha. I also had a vague feeling I had seen hime earlier.

'The burglar?' she said, her mouth open.

'He's obviously not a burglar! He must be a guest or something.'

The man spoke to Suman, who looked slightly disinterested. 'Anyway, I'm going out,' he said. She waved him away.

We saw him again the following day. He was wearing the same clothes as before and he was watching TV, his legs up on the dining room table. This time, he smiled at Mahrukh, who was fetching us tea from the kitchen.

'I'm sure I've seen him somewhere before,' said Mahrukh.

'Who was that man?' asked Ayesha, when we were resting in the garden after we had climbed up yet another hill with Suman.

'Which man?'

'The one who was in your house.'

'Oh, Rishiraj? He's one of those relatives I was telling you about. I guess he would be some kind of nephew. He was supposed to leave ages ago, with the others, but he's still here. Says he wants to take advantage of our lovely family home. I wish he would go back, though, he leaves everything in a mess and never cleans up after himself.'

'I saw him that day. When we were ... you know,' I said.

'Trespassing on my property?'

'Yes.'

'Good thing he didn't see you!'

'Why is that a good thing?' asked Ayesha.

'Because, being the bigmouths that you all are, you would have told him why you were there. Rishiraj doesn't know that the journal is missing. I haven't told him, and I don't plan to.'

'Why not?'

Suman sat up. 'Remember I told you how some of the members of my family didn't like my grandmother? And how some of my uncles and aunts were still really mad about the school?' We all nodded. 'Well, Rishiraj's one of the people who still think the family money shouldn't have gone to waste. His father, who is some kind of second cousin or something, didn't like that we were letting all Madhavi's journals stay in the school, and neither does he. His father was really mad at me for insisting they stay there.'

'Why do they want the journals?' asked Mahrukh. 'Do they want to read them?'

'They'd never read them! They're just angry that all the family stuff is not with the family. Besides, my grandmother wrote a lot about the fights that the family was having. They think that stuff should remain private. I said no. Let people know about it all!' Suman threw her hands up in the air. 'Seriously, though, she put her entire life into that school and her family was never nice to her, at least not until she was very, very old. I don't think her things belong to them at all, and I told them so. I wasn't terribly popular with them for it,' she said, sighing, but not unhappily.

'So is it a *very* big deal that I lost the journal?' I asked, my lip quivering.

'Not a very big deal at all,' she said kindly. 'I've just managed not to fight with them for a long time, so why bother telling them?'

'That's true,' said Mahrukh sagely.

'Why didn't we see Rishiraj last week?' asked Ayesha.

'He's been out a lot, thank god,' said Suman. 'Now stop asking questions and irritating me. I'm old. I want to take a nap.' She shut her eyes.

'I'm *sure* I've seen him somewhere,' said Mahrukh.

A few days later, we were in the library, trying desperately to find books to use for our project. 'I can't believe they're making us do this!' said Maitreyi, who was getting frustrated. 'There's no way that we'll be able to do our project with just these books.' It was a fitting punishment, since we had lost the only one we really wanted to use.

'We should ask if we can use the internet,' said Ayesha. 'We're not allowed, but Elizabeth and Mahrukh will be able to, from their homes.' She looked at us jealously.

'No internet for me,' said Mahrukh sadly. That was her punishment at home. 'You're our only hope, Elizabeth.'

'All right,' I said. 'But that doesn't mean I'm doing all the work.'

'Of course it does,' said Ayesha, smiling to herself. 'I vote Elizabeth does all the work.' I stuck my tongue out at her. Maitreyi poked me hard.

'Ow, Maitreyi, there was no need for that ...' I began, but she motioned for me to shut up and pointed at the librarian's desk.

A scruffy-looking man had just walked in and was talking to Miss Z. It was Rishiraj, Suman's nephew.

'Of course you can have a look at them!' Miss Z was saying. 'You're family, after all.'

'Actually, there's just one I'm interested in ...' he said, and his voice trailed off as they went into the inner room, where all the important things were kept.

'Do you think it's our book?' Maitreyi asked, looking at us.

'No, it can't be the same one,' I told her. 'Suman said he doesn't know, and it's not even one of the really important ones.'

We waited until they came out. Miss Z was apologising

profusely and Rishiraj was yelling. 'This is preposterous!' he was saying. 'Just wait! I'm going to make sure you don't see a single one of those journals again.' He sounded threatening.

'We'll have it back soon,' she said. 'There's really nothing to worry about.'

'Have it back by Monday,' Rishiraj said. 'I need to see it. Those journals are not yours to give away,' he said, wagging his finger at her.

He left the library in a huff, and Miss Z sank into her chair.

I went up to her. 'Miss, what happened?' I asked eventually.

'You saw what happened!' she said in despair. 'It's just our luck. He wants exactly the book that I lent you. Now I've gone and told him we'll have it back soon. I don't know what we're going to do.'

'You told him we had taken the journal?' I asked, slightly afraid. We would be going back to that house in a couple of days, and I did not like the look of his temper.

'I didn't tell him anything about where it was, just that it had been borrowed by some students. When he comes back, I will have to tell him it is lost and then the whole family will know and all those annoying people will make so much trouble for us. *Just* our luck.'

'Why did you tell him you'll have it back by Monday?' I asked, feeling really, really awful.

'He's threatening to sue us,' she said. 'Saying that if, I can't show it to him on Monday, he's going to report that we can't take care of them properly, and that they should be returned. I thought it might buy us some time to decide what to do.' She rushed off in search of Palak Nanda.

I was very confused. Suman had said she wasn't going to say anything to him. But if she hadn't, he wouldn't have known that the book was missing. And she couldn't have told him that we'd lost it, because he wouldn't be asking to see it by Monday. Monday was in two days.

I went out to talk to the others, who were standing outside the library, whispering to each other.

'I remember where I've seen Rishiraj before!' said Mahrukh excitedly. 'I heard his voice and I remembered.'

'Where?' I asked.

'At my shop, don't you remember? He was standing around near us the whole time, and he was listening to our conversation and laughing at something stupid. And I told him to go away. He was right next to us!'

'The biscuit guy!' I said. Suddenly, everything made sense. 'Okay, we need an emergency project meeting at once.'

We went back to the bench near the basketball court, which had become our standard meeting place during lunchtime. I told them everything Miss Z had said to me.

'It's Rishiraj,' said Ayesha.

'What?'

'It's him. He took it.'

'Not this again ...' began Maitreyi.

'She's right,' I said, stopping her. 'Look. There was only one person who knew about the book apart from us and Miss Z, and that was Suman. We *know* she hasn't taken it. And he *was* listening in on our conversation that day, I remember now.'

'Which means that Rishiraj knew we had the journal, and if he had been in the house that day, he must have taken it!' said Maitreyi, understanding at last. 'He's using that book to get all the others back. This is horrible, and it's all our fault!'

'My fault!' I whimpered.

'Would you just *shut up,*' snarled Mahrukh. 'Okay, this time we're really getting the book back.'

'Can you tell Miss Z that we saw him?' Maitreyi asked me.

'She won't believe us, none of them will,' said Ayesha.

'We have to at least tell Suman,' I said.

'We can't do that,' said Mahrukh. 'We've already broken into her house once and accused her of stealing the journal. Now we can't just tell her her nephew stole the book.'

'So what do we do now?' asked Maitreyi. 'You know, she doesn't like him and she might believe us ...'

Mahrukh looked at her. 'You know, I really don't think that's going to happen. What we should do is break into her house again.'

'No!' Maitreyi and I shouted at the same time.

We argued about whether or not to do it for half an hour. Then we argued about how to do it, and finally about who would do what. Like that, our second plan was made.

15

I was standing in Suman Sultania's kitchen when the sheer recklessness of our plan finally hit me. I couldn't even begin to imagine the kind of trouble we would be in if we got caught this time. The argument that finally got me to agree, cunningly put forward by Mahrukh, was that we owed it to Miss Z, who was going to be in plenty of trouble because of us.

'We're clearing our names,' said Ayesha, who must have guessed what I was thinking. 'Even prisoners get to clear their names.' She was looking through the kitchen drawers, taking an unnecessary amount of trouble to put all the forks and spoons back exactly as they had been.

'Not by doing exactly the same thing they went to prison for,' I pointed out. 'Why would he have hidden anything in the kitchen?'

'You never know.'

Now that we knew Rishiraj was staying in the house, we could figure out that his room was probably the one we had found locked the last time. It was still locked. None of the other rooms, except what was clearly Suman's bedroom, seemed to have anyone staying in them. We were certain that the journal was in his room, so what we had to do was to look for a spare key. We knew that there had to be at least one somewhere—Suman had told us one day that because she lost keys a lot, she always had many copies of every key made—but we had no idea where she kept it.

Maitreyi and Mahrukh had quickly claimed the bedrooms to search. Ayesha was left with the kitchen and living room, and I, for some reason, was trailing stupidly behind her.

'I don't think we're going to find anything here,' she finally admitted. We went upstairs to see how the other two were doing.

We walked into Suman's room to see Mahrukh rummaging in the cupboard. 'Nothing yet,' she declared. 'I checked all her pockets.' The cupboard was a complete mess.

'Are you mental?' asked Ayesha. 'You've got to tidy this up, she's *so* going to notice that someone was in here.'

'It was already like this,' said Mahrukh defensively. 'I didn't mess it up. Her room is *really* untidy!'

We went to the library which was being searched by Maitreyi, who was having a wonderful time. Unfortunately, Maitreyi wasn't having much luck looking for the spare keys, any more than we had had looking for the journal last time.

Suddenly, we heard a noise, like a door opening. *Not again*, I thought, as the feeling of terror, now familiar, spread through me.

'Is he back?' asked Maitreyi, in a whisper.

'I'm not hiding this time,' I said, resolutely.

'Yes, you are,' said Maitreyi, pushing me into a corner and shutting the door to the library as softly as she could.

'I'll scream,' I warned her.

'Good idea, Elizabeth,' she said, in a tone she could only have learned from her mother.

The door slammed a second time, and I guessed that a second person had come into the house as well. We could hear raised voices—Suman Sultania was clearly in the middle of an argument with her nephew.

'This is *not* your decision to make,' she was saying, sounding furious.

'We'll let the lawyer decide that,' shouted Rishiraj. 'You're not doing as great a job as you claim, that's obvious. That librarian told me everything. You knew that they were losing our things and you didn't say a word.'

I looked around and saw the expressions on the others' faces. They were obviously thinking the same thing as I was. I listened more carefully, because Suman's voice had gone quieter as she got angrier.

'I want you out of my house,' she said. 'I think you should leave as soon as possible.'

'Don't worry,' Rishiraj said. 'I'm leaving soon.' We could hear him walk out of the living room and up the stiars. There was the sound of a door opening and shutting.

'Okay, this is enough,' I said. 'We've got to go.'

The others opened their mouths to argue, but there wasn't time. The door to the library opened, and we saw a dark figure standing in the passageway. Ayesha began to squeal so I hit her.

'You've *got* to be joking,' the dark figure said, in Suman Sultania's voice. She was looking extremely unhappy.

Maitreyi and Ayesha jumped in, trying to explain, all at once. Suman stared.

'Sorry. We were just leaving,' said Mahrukh, helplessly. 'We'll never come back. Ever. We promise.'

'What's wrong with the four of you?' asked Suman, obviously as mad as hell but also genuinely confused. 'Why won't you leave me alone?'

'Miss Z never told Rishiraj,' I blurted out.

'What?'

'She never told him anything about the book. I was there.'

She looked at me, trying to understand. Mahrukh began to explain everything to her, slowly. She cut Mahrukh off. 'You're all mad.'

'We thought he had taken it,' I said. 'We're really sorry. We'll go.' I was on the verge of tears.

Suman waved to me to stop talking. She thought for a moment.

'He'd never let me go in there,' she said slowly.

'We can,' Ayesha told her encouragingly. I poked her hard and shook my head.

Suman glared at all of us, walked out of the and called out to her nephew as she went down. A minute later, we heard Rishiraj come out of his room, and walk down the stairs. Suman started talking to him loudly in the kitchen.

Mahrukh dashed out quietly and came back in a few seconds. 'His door's unlocked,' she said. 'I'm going in. Who's coming with me?'

'Let's not,' I pleaded. 'She's going to be so mad.'

'She wants us to go in!' said Ayesha. 'You heard her!'

'No, she doesn't,' I argued.

'I'm coming with you,' said Maitreyi. She looked at Ayesha and me. 'The bedrooms are ours. We agreed.'

'That's a good idea,' said Ayesha, obviously relieved. 'Elizabeth and I will keep watch.'

They left silently, and Ayesha and I waited nervously. Suddenly, we heard Rishiraj come back up and walk down to the passage to his room. He went in. I grabbed Ayesha's hand, hard. We waited for something to happen, but nothing did. That is, until he came out of his room and locked it again.

'We have to go!' shouted Suman from the living room.

Ayesha and I waited for what felt like ages even after we heard the front door slam. 'They're probably dead,' she breathed. 'He must have strangled them, quietly.'

'Don't be silly,' I whispered back through gritted teeth, not entirely convinced that she was wrong.

We crept into the living room. Suman and Rishiraj were definitely gone. I immediately went and checked the back door. It was latched, not locked. We weren't stuck like the last time. At least, Ayesha and I weren't. We still had no way to get the other two out. I tried to prepare myself to go and recruit the help of our parents once more, but when I turned around, Ayesha was grinning.

'Told you she wanted us to,' she said, holding up a large keyring with some twenty keys on it.

'Where did you find those?' I asked her, gaping.

'On the table. She must have left them here.'

'So annoying! If only we had found this before!'

We quickly ran up to Rishiraj's room and, after trying half a dozen keys, the door.

Maitreyi and Mahrukh were nowhere to be seen. I panicked.

'They're gone,' wailed Ayesha. 'He did kill them!'

A head poked out from under the bed and told her to shut up. It belonged to Maitreyi. She and Mahrukh crawled out, all dusty.

I was the one who found the journal. By then, we had been looking for quite a long time, and I had begun to think that he had maybe thrown it away or destroyed it. But there it was, wrapped in some clothes in the cupboard.

I had never felt such a massive sense of relief in my life. I hugged it tightly, and the others were jumping up and down in joy, squealing.

'Let's go give it back to Miss Z!' shouted Mahrukh, over our happy screams.

'She won't be at school on a Sunday,' I told them. 'And I don't know where she lives.'

'We'll give it to her tomorrow,' said Maitreyi. 'Imagine how happy she's going to be!'

'No,' I told them firmly. 'We're not keeping it a day longer.'

We ran out of the house towards the bus stop. The entire way to town, I held the book firmly to my chest, and didn't let anyone else touch it.

When we got off the bus, we ran all the way to school, and to Palak Nanda's office. She was fast asleep at her desk and I felt a strange sort of affection for her when I peered through the window. Her head was leaning against the back of her chair, her mouth was wide open and she was drooling. Open in front of her, on the desk, was a copy of her own book.

Ayesha banged on the door so hard that she almost fell off her chair. She opened the door, looking slightly fearful and obviously wondering what new awful thing she was going to have to deal with.

I handed her the journal silently, and her expression immediately changed.

16

By the end of the term, we had finally finished our project, under the watchful eye of Miss Z. I had redeemed myself somewhat, after the finding of the book, but we still weren't allowed to use it alone. We didn't have time to go and talk to all the people we wanted to, so we cancelled our initial idea for the project, and decided to write a paper on Madhavi Sultania instead.

Both Tanveen Miss and Miss Z agreed to let us look at the other journals as long as Palak Nanda was okay with it. Palak Nanda had been eaten up with guilt for having accused us of losing the journal, so she agreed.

'I'm *so* glad this is over,' she had told us, after an unnecessarily formal apology in her office. 'You must have all been feeling so *bad*. To not be trusted is a *terrible* thing.'

'It's okay, miss, really,' I said, feeling extremely uncomfortable. Suman Sultania had told Palak Nanda everything, trying to focus on the getting-the-book-back part and not so much on the breaking-into-her-house-again part. We were all very grateful for this.

'Which is not to say, of course, that everything you did was *okay*. I was very dismayed at your lack of respect for Ms Sultania's privacy. I hope you *never* do that sort of thing again.'

'Never, miss,' I said, and I really, really meant it.

The last day of school was also Open Day, which meant that our parents were all coming to school to meet the teachers. My parents were a lot more nervous than I was, given all that had happened during the term.

'Don't worry,' I told them, before I left that morning. 'No one's mad at me anymore.'

'Who knows,' muttered my mother. 'Who knows, these days, what you're up to?'

I gave up trying to reassure them. 'See you soon,' I said, and left quickly.

Mahrukh, Maitreyi, Ayesha and I were going to visit Suman Sultania afterwards. The stuff about the journals had just been sorted out—they were being moved out of the school after all, but it was good, she said. The books were going to be in the Lailapani Public Library where anyone could go and look at them whenever they wanted. She was in a great mood, because Rishiraj was so angry at being accused of taking the book that he swore he'd never come back to visit her again. And she was sure he would not try to mess with the school again. She'd invited us for tea to celebrate.

'She's going to make us go hiking again,' said Ayesha, pulling a face. 'I don't want to go.'

The rest of us had been trying for a couple of weeks to figure out what exactly was going on with Ayesha. She had been in a strange mood.

'You like going to Suman's house,' offered Maitreyi.

'Whatever,' said Ayesha. 'Anyway, I have to pack for home.'

After much discussion, Maitreyi, Mahrukh and I hadn't been able to decide whether Ayesha was happy or sad about the fact that she was going back to Delhi for the winter holidays. She would go on and on about how happy she was to get out of this horrible place. She said she missed her computer, and her house. But whenever we talked about what we were going to do over the holidays, she would sulk and make an excuse to leave. After much discussion, we decided to leave it alone, mostly because Ayesha was scary when she was sulking.

She was in a particularly bad mood on Open Day because her parents had come into town a day earlier, to meet all the teachers and to take her home.

'Is it compulsory, though?' Maitreyi asked her. 'Couldn't you have told them not to come?'

'I tried,' said Ayesha. 'They wanted to come. Especially after they heard about everything that happened.'

'They know about everything?' I asked.

'Of course they know. Palak Nanda called and told them.'

So that's why she was worried, I thought. She was scared of getting into trouble again, like she did at her last school. Oddly, the thought of her having to leave Hill School after all felt slightly unpleasant.

'It's okay,' Maitreyi told her. 'Everything's fine now. Palak Nanda will tell them that it turned out fine. Won't she?' she asked us, worried.

'If she doesn't forget,' Mahrukh said, unhelpfully. Ayesha

just shrugged.

We didn't have any classes that day. There was assembly, where Palak Nanda spoke for a very long time about all the feelings that she had had during the term, and some kids from Class V and Class VI sang a song. At the end, Palak Nanda thanked us for our patience and cooperation, which was weird.

Later, all the parents came to school.

'Which ones are yours?' I asked Ayesha. She pointed to a smartly dressed couple in a heated conversation with Palak Nanda, who was looking trapped.

'You look just like your mother,' observed Mahrukh.

Ayesha made a face. Just then, her parents noticed her and waved to her to join them. She walked off unwillingly.

I found my parents and headed to our classroom with them. The desks were all set up so that we could go and talk to the teachers, one by one.

I looked around, wondering where to start. I was the most worried about Indu Miss. I looked over to her desk, where she was talking to some other girl's parents. 'We don't like to use the word *fail* in this school,' she was saying. 'However, as you can see ...'

I quickly ushered my parents over to Shabnam Miss's corner of the room. At least, I was still doing well at maths. Shabnam Miss smiled broadly as she saw them coming.

It wasn't compulsory for us for to be there, so I told my parents I'd be back and went outside, where Ayesha and Maitreyi were hanging around.

'How'd it go?' I asked Ayesha.

'Fine,' she said, though she was looking miffed. 'My parents apologised a lot to Palak Nanda, and she said it's okay. They want to speak to Suman and say sorry for my behaviour.'

'That's not so bad,' I assured her.

The rest of the day went by comfortably. Even my parents' meeting with Indu Miss wasn't a complete disaster. She told them about the essay that I was supposed to write for her, which I had completely forgotten about, and added snidely that perhaps I had been too busy with some other events.

When everything was finally done, the four of us set off for Suman Sultania's house. Ayesha had lied to her parents, saying that she was coming over to my place, because she was worried that they might try to come along to meet Suman.

Maitreyi was staying on for the vacation. Indu Miss was going to stay on to help Palak Nanda prepare for the next term. I had no plans at all.

I thought briefly of Pallavi. I never really got to do much during the winter break, because my father had to work and my mother had a very short amount of time off so sometimes they'd let me go on vacation with Pallavi and her parents. They'd go on day trips sometimes, and take me along, but mostly we'd just spend the vacation at each other's houses. This would be the first winter in years that she wasn't going to be around at all. I decided not to think about it.

Ayesha was leaving the next day so we were going to have a slumber party at my house that night. Ayesha's parents had grudgingly agreed to let her stay over. My own parents, of course, were thrilled that I was having people over and had prepared excitedly for our slumber party by pulling out all the spare blankets and mattresses.

As soon as we neared her gate, Suman shouted at us from the garden. 'Just in time! What a perfect day for a walk, no excuses. Ayesha, your parents called me and I've already told them how lazy you are!'

'They *called* you?' Ayesha sounded mortified.

'They wanted to come and see me, but I told them I was busy today, meeting some old friends,' Suman told Ayesha, who beamed at her adoringly.

It was not the perfect day for a walk, at all. Even though the sun was out, it was beginning to get extremely cold. When I mentioned this to Suman, she simply told me a brisk walk would warm us up and stuffed some extra shawls into her bag.

'Are you looking forward to your holidays?' Suman asked us as we went up.

'I'm not. The rest of them are all making plans without me,' said Ayesha.

'You probably have plans too, without us,' I told her.

'Of course she does! She used her mother's phone today, to send a bunch of emails to her friends. Her *other* friends,' said Maitreyi. 'And Mahrukh's going to be away, visiting her sister at college. So it's just Elizabeth and me here for the winter break.'

'You can always come and visit,' said Suman. She swatted a mosquito that was sitting on Maitreyi's head.

'You can come and visit me too,' I said to Maitreyi. 'You can come and stay with me.'

'Can I? I'll be stuck at the hostel the whole time, otherwise. I'll only have my mother, and you, and ... well, just my mother and you, for company. I'm sure there'll be hardly anyone else.'

'You can go exploring and stuff,' Mahrukh offered.

'Yes, so the next time you abandon us in the woods, at least we'll know the way back,' I told her.

'Or next time, we can leave *you* there,' said Maitreyi, who was still a little sore about the whole thing. She shoved Mahrukh, who put some dried leaves in her hair.

'Here we are!' shouted Suman, before Maitreyi could retaliate.

She had taken us to a clearing, where we sat down and ate the chicken puffs that Mahrukh's mum had sent with her for Suman. We hung out there for almost two hours.

As Ayesha and Mahrukh chatted with Suman and Maitreyi dozed off in the sun, I sat and thought. I was looking forward to hanging out with Maitreyi and doing Christmas things and generally having things to do when I had been expecting to be bored out of my mind. But I couldn't help hoping, a little meanly, that Pallavi would have a bad Christmas trip with her school. Then maybe she'd come back for the whole summer. She probably thought I didn't want to see her anyway, because I hadn't written to her after all.

'We should go before it gets dark,' Suman said finally. 'I don't want your parents to be worried.'

The bus ride back home was all about plans for our

slumber party. Maitreyi and Ayesha kept talking about dinner and midnight snacks, which was strange until you realised they had been eating mess and canteen food for an entire term.

We got home, set up the mattresses and were in our night clothes by 9 pm. We had been sitting and chatting for about an hour when I heard my mother calling my name.

'What?' I yelled.

She said nothing so I went outside in a huff. She handed me the phone.

'Who is it?' I asked, though I could guess. 'How's your trip?' I asked Pallavi icily.

'I said I *might* go, you idiot, not that I would.'

'So where are you?'

'At my *house*.'

'What? Why didn't you tell me?' I asked.

'I just got back an hour ago. And I didn't write to you because what's the point? Then I thought I'd surprise you. Then I thought about it and got angry with you. Then my mother made me call you.'

'I've been really busy,' I told her guiltily.

'Yes? Doing what? I know you're lying. Your mother told me you're having a sleepover,' she said.

'*So* many things have happened!' I burst out. 'The principal is crazy and I had to play hide-and-seek on Sports Day and I caught a thief, you won't believe it, and I'm sorry I didn't write to you or tell you anything but I don't know why I didn't,' I ended breathlessly.

'What? I can't understand anything you're saying,' she said. Then she called out loudly to her mother. 'Can I go to Elizabeth's house?'

I was nervous about Pallavi meeting the others, especially since I had never even mentioned her to them. She and Mahrukh knew each other, of course, but not very well.

'How's your new school?' Mahrukh asked her when she arrived shortly after.

'Nice, I guess. Very normal. My mother's very happy with it. My mother says Hill School has gone to the dogs.'

'It hasn't!' objected Maitreyi.

'She's a bit strange,' Pallavi reassured her. 'So who's going to tell me what's been going on?'

A. Coven is a hybrid creature. Filmmaker, author, editor and philosopher, she has been to many schools across the country. Her Pathan-Bihari-Mallu-Bong genes and her pan-Indian upbringing make her multilingual and the perfect citizen of Delhi, except that she doesn't live there any more.